What had happened to Ben that he needed this break from his job as an E.R. doctor?

From what Shannon saw in his expression she sensed it was more than stress.

She held his gaze, her puzzlement growing. Then, to her dismay, she felt it again. That faint trickle of awareness fingering her spine, followed by the sensation of attraction she hadn't felt in a long time.

For the tiniest moment she wanted to allow it to grow. To allow that little thrill of anticipation, the kind she hadn't felt since Arthur, to begin.

And look where that got you.

Her practical sense intervened, thankfully, and quashed her utter foolishness. Getting involved with a guy was silly and futile, especially someone as closely connected to her former fiancé as Ben was.

Books by Carolyne Aarsen

Love Inspired

A Bride at Last
The Cowboy's Bride
†*A Family-Style Christmas*
†*A Mother at Heart*
†*A Family at Last*
A Hero for Kelsey
Twin Blessings
Toward Home
Love Is Patient
A Heart's Refuge
Brought Together by Baby
A Silence in the Heart
Any Man of Mine
Yuletide Homecoming
Finally a Family
A Family for Luke
The Matchmaking Pact
Close to Home
Cattleman's Courtship
Cowboy Daddy
The Baby Promise
**The Rancher's Return*
The Cowboy's Lady
*Daddy Lessons
**Healing the Doctor's Heart*

†Stealing Home
*Home to Hartley Creek

CAROLYNE AARSEN

and her husband, Richard, live on a small ranch in northern Alberta, where they have raised four children and numerous foster children, and are still raising cattle. Carolyne crafts her stories in an office with a large west-facing window through which she can watch the changing seasons while struggling to make her words obey.

Healing the Doctor's Heart

Carolyne Aarsen

Love Inspired

Recycling programs
for this product may
not exist in your area.

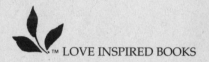

™ LOVE INSPIRED BOOKS

ISBN-13: 978-0-373-81626-2

HEALING THE DOCTOR'S HEART

Copyright © 2012 by Carolyne Aarsen

www.LoveInspiredBooks.com

Printed in U.S.A.

Guide me in your truth and teach me, for you are God my Savior and my hope is in you all day long.
—*Psalms* 25:5

With many thanks to Shauntelle Nelson,
who let me borrow her coffee shop, Mug Shots,
for this series. If you're ever in Fernie, B.C.,
stop in and make sure to try the banana loaf.

Chapter One

"Really, Nana? This is the house you want to buy?" Shannon Deacon wrapped her arms around her midsection, frowning at the older Craftsman house tucked against tall fir trees. Its low-pitched roof, wide eaves and heavy beams supporting the spacious deck created an air both welcoming and solid, a feeling Shannon knew her nana treasured.

"I'm tired of looking around," Nana Beck said as she got out of Shannon's car. "This house and yard are big enough for all my grandchildren and future great-grandchildren. Now that you've let your lease run out on your apartment, there's lots of room for you to stay with me until you…until after Carter and Emma's wedding."

Shannon didn't miss the hesitation in her grandmother's last sentence. They both knew that a few weeks after Shannon's last duty as bridesmaid for her friend Emma was done, she was taking a holiday and after that, starting a new job in a large Chicago hospital almost two thousand miles from Nana, her cousins and Hartley Creek, British Columbia.

"But why here? In this neighborhood?" Shannon continued. *And why a house beside Sophie Brouwer's?*

Shannon's gaze drifted unwillingly to the starkly modern home sitting on an unbroken expanse of lawn a few hundred feet away. Less than a year ago Sophie Brouwer had been on the verge of becoming her mother-in-law. Then her son Arthur had dumped Shannon two weeks before their wedding and now the sight of that house was a painful and embarrassing reminder of the past.

Nana patted her shoulder. "Honey, I didn't move next door to Arthur's mother on purpose. This house really was the only one I wanted. Besides, you are well over Arthur by now and you're better off without him."

"So you keep saying."

"Don't worry, honey. You'll find someone else," Nana consoled her.

"I don't want to find anyone else," Shannon said, unable to keep the sharpness out of her voice. "I have no intention of making myself that vulnerable again. Ever."

Her nana's surprised look made Shannon regret her angry tone. Shannon dragged her hands over her face, feeling the heavy funk of sleep deprivation. She knew it had as much to do with her mood as her nana's choice to live next door to her ex-fiancé's mother. Shannon had just come off a hectic twelve-hour shift in the emergency department of Hartley Creek Hospital and her head still buzzed. She didn't get a break until her shift ended.

Shannon held the door open for her grandmother just as her cell phone sent out its happy chimes. She glanced at the number and her heart sank. The hospital. "I'll just be a minute," she said. "I'll meet you inside."

"Don't be too long," Nana warned. "I want to go downtown after this to put in an offer on the house."

Shannon nodded, then pushed a button to connect the call. "Shannon here," she said into the phone, just as a large diesel truck pulled up behind her grandmother's car. The driver stopped, stretched his arms out in front of him, then pulled his hands over his face. He looked as tired as Shannon felt.

His features created a thud in her chest, but as he adjusted his cap, she caught a glimpse of dark hair instead of blond. Brown eyes instead of blue.

Not Arthur, thank goodness, she thought as her heart slowed its heavy beat, but this man's face, though obscured by a cap, still teased out a memory.

"You'll be glad to know I got your shift covered for tomorrow," her colleague Daphne was saying over the phone. "But I really need you to work the rest of the week."

Shannon felt a heavy weariness fall on her at the thought of having to work again in thirty-six hours after six twelve-hour shifts in a row.

"You do realize I'm only supposed to work three shifts a week until I quit," she said, glancing at the truck again still trying to figure out why the driver looked familiar.

"If it's any consolation Doc Henneson has been going steady for the past week and so has Doc Shuster as well as Dr. Martin. Sure wish we could find another doctor willing to work out here."

"Poor guys. That is some consolation," Shannon said. "I guess I'll see you in thirty-six hours then. Take care." Shannon ended the call and blew out an exhausted breath. The hospital had been running short staffed for the past couple of months, which made Shannon feel even more guilty about quitting and moving away. But she had made her mind up. She would have left this town sooner, but her grandmother's heart attack shortly after the canceled wedding had made her postpone her plans. Then her cousin's own wedding made her postpone her plans again. But after that, she was out of here.

She dropped her phone in her pocket just as the driver of the truck, who now had his back to her, pulled a box out of the back. Then he turned.

Shannon felt a pain in her chest as the memories clicked into place.

The dark hair worn short, the deep-set brown eyes, the eyebrows like two dark slashes across the bridge of his forehead, his unsmiling mouth and the cleft in his chin all combined to create a cruel twist in her heart.

From the first time she had met Ben Brouwer, Arthur's older brother, she'd been struck by the differences between the two brothers. While Arthur was blond, blue eyed and outgoing, Ben was dark, taciturn and, if she was honest, a bit intimidating. A curious trait for an emergency-room doctor.

Ben shifted the box, then looked up. He pulled back, as if he'd been hit, taking a step backward. Then he recovered and sauntered up the walk.

"Hello, Shannon," he said, his deep voice reverberating in the quiet of the neighborhood.

The afternoon sun cast his face in shadow,

making him look even more stern. As he came nearer she saw his eyes fringed with thick, dark lashes and in their brown depths she caught a glimpse of pain and regret.

The same pain and regret she'd seen in his eyes a year ago when he had come to her apartment to tell her that his brother, Arthur, Shannon's fiancé, was calling off the wedding and had already left town.

Shannon wondered if Ben had given her another thought after throwing his horrible, life-changing news into her life, then leaving. She wondered if he regretted covering for his cowardly brother.

And then, as their gazes met and clung, in spite of her memories, a hint of attraction budded in her dormant heart.

No. This wasn't happening. Not a chance. Hadn't she learned her lesson?

She swallowed and gave him a tight nod, her arms wrapped around her midsection, as if protecting herself from her own renegade emotions.

"Visiting your mother?" she asked, pleased she could sound so casual around this man who had been the chief spectator of her total humiliation.

Ben looked down at the box he held and shook his head. "Actually, no. I'm moving in."

Shannon blinked, surprised and confused at

his words. "But I thought you worked…thought you were a doctor in Ottawa working in the emergency department."

"I'm taking time away from work," he said, the cold note in his voice creating an answering chill in Shannon. "Helping my mother do some much-needed work on her house and yard."

"I see." But she didn't. Surely he could hire someone to do the work instead of taking time away from an important job?

"And why are you here?" he asked in the brusque voice she easily remembered from before.

"My nana— grandmother," she added, "she's moving from my cousin Carter's ranch into town and looking for a house. She seems to be attached to this one."

She wasn't imagining the deepening of Ben Brouwer's frown or the thinning of his lips. He seemed to have the same opinion of her grandmother's choice that she had, though why he cared she didn't know.

"Isn't it a bit large for her?" he asked.

"It's a *lot* large for her but she does have a lot of family. Anyway, it's still up in the air." Now that she knew Ben Brouwer would be living next door, as well, Shannon knew she wasn't moving in with her nana. There was no way she wanted to see Ben Brouwer every day.

Or, worse yet, run the risk of seeing his brother.

Ben's only reply was a curt nod. "I hope she finds something that works for her."

Then his features softened and his eyes caught hers again. "And how have you been?"

His words, so quiet, so mundane, rested between them, weighted with the past.

The muted sounds of the town surrounded them. A hopeful bird sent out a sweet song, looking for a mate. The swish of vehicles on other streets, the cries of people in other yards. In the distance the train sent out its melancholy clarion call. All the sounds threaded through each other reminding Shannon that life moved on.

Shannon drew in a slow breath, trying to measure her words. Though she wasn't sure why it mattered, she didn't want this man to think her life had been defined by his brother's broken promises.

Even though it had.

"I'm good. I've… I've got a job in Chicago starting in a couple of months."

His frown deepened. "So you're leaving Hartley Creek?"

She nodded.

"But I thought you loved it here."

And as Arthur's brother, he would know. The fact that Shannon had wanted to stay in this town after she and Arthur were married had been a source of tension between them. In fact, as soon as Arthur had called off the wedding, he had moved away.

"Things change."

Ben's expression grew even more serious and in his eyes Shannon saw something that created a curl of anger in her midsection.

Pity.

"I'm so—"

"I hope you enjoy your stay with your mother." She cut him off midsympathy. She didn't want this man's pity. "I'm sure she'll enjoy having you around."

Thankfully he got the hint and simply nodded his reply.

They endured an awkward moment of silence; then Shannon poked her thumb over her shoulder. "I better have a look inside."

And before he could say anything more, she turned and walked away, resisting the urge to shoot another look over her shoulder. Ben Brouwer was just another man and she wasn't interested in any man.

Especially not one who had been the instrument of so much pain and sorrow.

She looked the same and yet so different. Ben watched Shannon walk to the door of the house, still wearing her brightly colored nurse scrubs.

Her auburn hair flowing down her back looked longer than he remembered and she had lost weight. Her face was narrower, and the smattering of freckles that his brother, Arthur, had always thought so cute were more pronounced against the paleness of her complexion. Her eyes had grown harder and she held her mouth a bit tighter, as if restraining her emotions.

But she was just as beautiful as the last time he'd seen her when he'd gone to her apartment to deliver the news his cowardly brother couldn't. News that Arthur had changed his mind and couldn't marry Shannon after all.

That day, as now, Shannon had been wearing her nurse's white shoes as she stood in the middle of the living room of her apartment, smoothing her hands down the front of the immaculately white wedding gown skimming her slender figure. Her younger sister, Hailey, knelt at her feet, pushing Shannon's hands away, fussing at her about getting stains on her dress only two weeks before her wedding. That day Shannon's wavy hair was pulled back away from a face flushed with anticipation.

She had looked so beautiful, Ben remembered. His younger brother's bride.

When he had come into Shannon's apartment, she had laughed with nervous excitement at his presence, reprimanding him for seeing her in her dress before the wedding. But her laughter died a hasty death when Ben delivered his news.

The dress she was trying on was unnecessary, he had to tell her. Arthur was calling off the wedding.

Shannon had stared at him, then emitted a nervous laugh. "Not funny," she told him.

And when she understood how serious he was, she had swayed and taken a stumbling step backward, reaching behind her for something, anything, to support her as she stammered out her questions.

Why? What had happened? What had she done wrong?

Hailey had caught Shannon, settled her down and then grabbed Ben, demanding an explanation. Ben stammered out a vague reply about Arthur being unsure for some time now about marrying Shannon and as the day came closer becoming more certain marrying Shannon wasn't right for him.

That was a year ago and at that time Ben had been a stressed-out, overworked emergency-room doctor in a relentlessly busy downtown Ottawa hospital, dealing with a cheating wife who wanted to end their marriage.

He wasn't supposed to come to Hartley until the day before the wedding. Then Arthur called him fifteen days early, asking Ben to please, please come and help him out. He needed his brother badly.

Ben heard the desperation in his brother's voice, called in some favors and shifted the time off he had booked for the wedding, then flew out to help his brother. Maybe even talk him out of what he was sure were prewedding jitters.

But when he got to Hartley Creek it was to discover Arthur had already skipped town, leaving Ben to finish what he couldn't.

Ben still got angry with Arthur when he thought about how easily he had ignored his responsibility to the woman who seemed so devoted to him.

After Ben returned to his job in Ottawa, and after his divorce was finalized, Ben caught himself thinking of Shannon from time to time. But he never called. He doubted she would appreciate contact with any of Arthur's relatives.

Ben adjusted the box he carried, then turned and walked back to his mother's house, putting the memories behind him.

He had his own problems right now. The biggest one was reminding himself to take life one day at a time, like his counselor told him.

As he came up the stairs of his mother's house,

she met him at the door, her arms open, her smile even wider. She wore her usual velour jogging suit and running shoes even though the fastest he'd ever seen his mother move was a casual stroll. Her hair, however, was immaculately coiffed, each strand positioned and shellacked so not a hair could shift until the spray was washed off.

"Here you are," she said, reaching her arms out to hug him. "I wondered when you were coming."

"I told you, Mother, four o'clock." He returned her hug with one arm, balancing the box of books with the other. "And here I am."

Sophie Brouwer reached up and stroked his cheek, then glanced past him to the large house beside hers. "Was that Shannon Deacon you were talking to? What is she doing here?"

"I think her grandmother might buy that house next door." Ben tossed the words out as if he wasn't bothered by the idea that he might see Shannon while he stayed here.

Right now he didn't need any distractions in his life. He wasn't looking any further than the two-month plan he had laid out when he'd asked for a leave of absence. His plans were simple. Help his mother finish the few odd jobs she wanted done in the house and on the yard. Give himself some space to reflect. Then decide what he would do.

"I'm sure Eloise Beck will make a lovely neighbor." Sophie took Ben by the arm and ushered him inside. "Though I can't imagine what she would want with such a big house."

Ben couldn't, either, but that was none of his business. "So where should I put my stuff?" he asked, shifting the increasingly heavy box in his arms.

"Oh, I'm sorry," his mother said with a quick clap of her hands. "Let me show you where you'll be staying. I don't know if you remember this house, but it will be the same room you were in when…" His mother let the words fade away and Ben knew she referred to Arthur's nonwedding. She fluttered her fingers as if erasing the memory. "Well, never mind that. You'll know where it is."

She ambled down the hallway toward the back of the house past a wall holding various pictures of Ben and Arthur over time.

Ben's steps slowed as he walked past a picture of his graduation from medical school. Such dreams he'd held then. Such plans to save the world.

Such a crock.

He followed his mother into the room she had prepared for him and looked around. "Looks good, Mom," he said, dropping his books on the bed. He walked to the window and gazed out over the expanse of yard and the work that lay ahead of him.

Downed trees lay in a crisscrossed mess at the back of the large property. The grass was overgrown and the hedge between his mother's house and the property beside hers looked like something out of a frightening fairy tale. The pond was a sludge of green overgrown with lilacs and weeds.

When his mother first moved here, Arthur had promised he would get it shipshape. Then Arthur shipped out and Ben hadn't had the time to come help.

"I know it looks like a lot of work, but you did say you'd be here a month," his mother said from behind him.

"That's the plan," Ben said, giving her a reassuring smile.

"And you'll be going back to Ottawa after that?"

Ben felt the steady beam of his mother's gaze and the weight of expectation behind it. His parents had invested heavily in his education. Not just monetarily but in terms of support and encouragement. He had been their shining star. The son who had made good and had become a doctor.

As opposed to Arthur, who, last he heard, was still working as a car salesman at yet another dealership.

Ben's gaze slid away from his mother's questioning one, and the sigh he released was heavy and ragged around the edges. "I'm not sure what's happening after this, Mother. I'm here to help you out and that's all I want to think of for now."

His mother laid her hand on his shoulder. "You've taken too much on," she said quietly. "You are a good doctor. You were doing your job. Saskia always asked too much of you."

Ben stretched out his clenched hands as if releasing the burdens he'd repeatedly picked up.

"I should have been there for her, Mother. She called me and I couldn't come. She was my wife."

"She *was* your wife," his mother reiterated. "You were divorced. She had no right to ask you to leave your work to go get her. You were busy. You were doing an important job."

His mind slipped back to the place he'd been avoiding for the past month.

"I was setting the broken arm of a murderer, Mother," he said, his voice bitter with regret and anger. "And because of that, my wife, my ex-wife, died."

Ben rested his hand against the cool glass of

the window. As he did he saw Shannon leaving the house with her grandmother. The sun caught auburn highlights in her hair, making it shimmer.

She was as beautiful as he remembered.

He checked his admiration.

Shannon was off-limits to him. Even if she and her grandmother did move next door, Shannon might as well be living on Mars.

He was a worn-out divorcee who had blown his chance at a relationship and she was his brother's ex-fiancée.

No way was anything ever possible between them.

Chapter Two

"This is not good." Shannon pulled a face as she looked up at the two-foot-wide gap in the wall of the living room. Pieces of old insulation spilled out of the hole and onto the carpet. She saw the edges of the shiplap covering the outside of the house.

The hole had been conveniently covered up with a picture the previous owners had left behind. Shannon and Nana had only just discovered the hole when they pulled the hideous velvet painting down.

When they had toured the house, Shannon had assumed the previous owners had forgotten about the picture. Because Nana was in such a hurry to buy the house, and because she didn't need a bank loan, she hadn't bothered getting an inspector to check it out.

The sale had been rushed. Now her grandmother owned this place and they were finding a few issues the real-estate agent conveniently hadn't mentioned.

This hole was in addition to a huge hole in the wall behind the stove. Nana had found that one when she set a trap to catch a mouse that had skittered across the floor when they moved in.

"You'll have to get Carter to have a look at this."

"He's too busy." Nana Beck's frown deepened as she tapped her manicured fingers against her lips. "I tried phoning some of the local contractors, but they're all booked up."

"What about Hailey's Dan? He sells building supplies, surely he would know something about fixing holes in walls?"

Nana just sighed. "I don't know how much of a carpenter he is. I don't even know how much work this would be."

"I wish you'd gotten an inspector to at least go over the house. He would have found these holes and the loose railing at the top of the stairs." And who knows what else.

"Thank goodness it's still spring and we don't have to worry too much about the cold weather for a while," Nana said, brightening, surprisingly upbeat about the whole debacle.

"We do have to worry about rain," Shannon grumbled, thinking about the roof shingles that had ended up on the lawn that morning after a nasty storm last night.

Nana gave Shannon a reassuring pat on her shoulder. "I'm sure it will all work out," she said. "Now let's get you moved into your room."

Shannon picked up one of her boxes and followed her grandmother, who carried some of Shannon's clothes, up the stairs. Nana opened the door and stepped into the room.

"I love how the sunshine comes in here," Nana said as she made a half turn in the beam of light spilling through the fly-specked window onto the wooden floor. "I think you'll be happy here," she said with a note of satisfaction. Shannon smiled at her grandmother's optimism as she ripped open the box she'd taped up only a couple of days ago.

"Even with the holes in the walls?"

"Those can be fixed," Nana said, her voice muffled as she hung Shannon's clothes up in the huge closet. She emerged, still smiling. "Even with the holes I still think this is better than you having to live in some stuffy apartment."

"Well, there wasn't a single stuffy apartment I could rent, anyway, and moving into Hailey's shoebox apartment wasn't an option." This was Shannon's best choice, which had seemed reasonable enough until she'd run into Ben. Shannon pulled her duvet out of the box and tossed it on the bed that Carter and Dan had already moved into the house.

All day yesterday, while Shannon was working at the hospital, her cousin Carter and his fiancée, Emma; Shannon's sister Hailey and her boyfriend, Dan; and Carter's hired hand, Wade, had moved her and Nana's earthly goods into the house.

For the most part, all her stuff was here. Only a few more boxes and she'd be done. It seemed pointless knowing she was moving in a couple of months again, but Shannon preferred to think of this move as a stopover in the process. A way to spend some time with her grandmother.

"In spite of all the other stuff, this house is so perfect for me," Nana Beck said, clasping her hands in front of her.

Shannon had to admit that much. Though it was large, as Ben Brouwer had so helpfully pointed out the last time she'd seen him, it was close enough to the hospital to give the family peace of mind. The doctor had warned Nana to be more careful after her heart attack over half a year ago. At the time, Nana Beck had been living out on Shannon's cousin Carter's ranch. Shannon felt that was too far from town and the hospital and had been pushing her to move into Hartley Creek. Thankfully Nana had agreed.

And now that Shannon's sister Hailey was

settling down in Hartley Creek, as well, this house could serve as a central meeting place for the family.

For the most part it was a good choice, the only exceptions being the holes and the neighbors who were a visible reminder of Arthur and the past.

Two months after getting Ben to deliver the news about the canceled wedding, Arthur had finally called Shannon. In halting words and incomplete sentences he'd told her their engagement had happened too quickly and had been a mistake. For the last months of their relationship he had felt as if he was going through the motions of love. He didn't feel like they were in sync anymore. She was always so solemn. So serious. As if she had taken on the weight of the world. He had foolishly thought getting engaged would ignite a spark he thought was missing from their relationship. But it hadn't. Then the wedding plans created a momentum he couldn't stop until just before the wedding.

Shannon jerked open the flaps on the top and bottom of the box, pushing away the memory. She shoved the box under the bed to join the other boxes she'd already emptied. She'd thought she had put all those old feelings away.

But now Arthur's brother and mother lived

next door and it was as if all the ground she had gained had been swept away.

"Why don't you throw those moving boxes away?" Nana asked with a frown. "You won't need them again."

Shannon tried not to roll her eyes. It was as if her nana thought ignoring the job in Chicago would make it mysteriously disappear.

Instead, Shannon brushed the dust off her pants and walked to the door. "Let's organize the kitchen and then I can finish unpacking my car."

Her nana didn't reply and Shannon glanced over her shoulder to see her grandmother looking out the window down at the street below.

"Nana? What do you think about doing the kitchen? Or are you too tired?"

Nana spun around, then waved her hands at Shannon in a shooing motion. "Oh, no. I'm not too tired at all. You go and get the boxes out of your car. I'll take care of the kitchen myself."

"I don't mind helping you."

Nana frowned. "I would just as soon do it on my own. Then I know where everything is." She flapped her hands again in Shannon's direction. "You run along. Hurry and get those boxes out of your car and then you don't have to think about that anymore. Just go."

Shannon nodded, puzzled at her grandmother's insistence, but shrugged it off as she headed down the hall to the wide stairs. As she had the first time she had toured this house, she paused at the landing halfway down, tracing the intricate lines of the stained-glass window set in the wall.

Naomi would love this, she thought, her heart contracting at the thought of her sister sitting vigil at her dying fiancé's bedside. Naomi had called a couple of days ago telling them it was a matter of weeks until Billy was gone.

Then she, too, would be returning to Hartley Creek.

One by one the family was coming together. First Carter, then Hailey. Soon Naomi. Garret, possibly.

But she, the one who had always stayed, the one who had never wanted to move away, would be leaving town shortly after Carter and Emma's wedding.

Melancholy brushed her soul as she fingered the necklace Nana had given her after her heart attack. A rough gold nugget in a setting hung from a thin gold chain. The nugget was a visible reminder of her and her cousins' past and of choices made by their ancestor, August Klauer. He had gone looking for gold but had come back looking for love.

Shannon shook the feeling aside, then walked the rest of the way down the stairs, trailing her hand over the wide banister of the stair. The stained-glass panels of the double doors at the end of the front hall were as dusty as the rest of the windows in this house, but they would show their true beauty once they were cleaned.

The living room off to the right side of the wide hallway held a jumble of furniture and boxes belonging to her grandmother, but the room on the other side was empty. The walls of this room held remnants of crayon marks and numerous dents and scuffs. Shannon guessed it had been, at one time, a playroom.

She cocked her head to one side, as if evoking the voices of the children who might have played here. The thought created a dull ache deep in her soul.

Would she ever have children? She pressed her hand to her abdomen as if imagining a child there. If she and Arthur had gotten married, they might have had a baby by now.

"Aren't you getting those boxes?" Nana's voice broke into her depressing thoughts and pulled her back from the brink of self-pity.

"Yeah. Sure," Shannon called back, puzzled at the urgency in her nana's voice. "Going right now."

She stepped out of the cool of the house into

the heat of the afternoon. A welcome heat, she thought, looking up at the mountains that still held a generous cap of snow. This year winter had hung around like an unwelcome guest hoping to tell another joke that no one wanted to hear.

But now it was gone and leaves had burst into glorious green, softening the branches of the birch and poplar trees lining the street.

She opened her car and was greeted by a blast of trapped heat. The tape on the largest box had curled away from the top and she carefully pulled it out, hoping it would hold together until she got it up to her bedroom.

She set it on the sidewalk, piled another box on top, hooked a couple of bags over her arm, bent over and lifted the whole business up.

"Need a hand?"

The deep voice behind her sent her heart into her throat and the boxes onto the ground. The curling tape released its precarious hold, the bottom box split open and its contents slithered out onto the sidewalk.

"Sorry. I didn't mean to scare you," Ben was saying as he knelt down to gather up the contents.

Please, Lord, don't let that box be holding my undergarments, Shannon prayed as she shot an agonized look over her shoulder. Then her heart flopped again when she saw Ben.

Ben's snug T-shirt enhanced the breadth of his shoulders and the muscles in his upper arms. His blue jeans were dusty and caked with dirt at the bottom and a bead of sweat tracked through the dust on his cheeks, yet he still looked very appealing.

"That's okay," she said, wishing her voice hadn't taken on that breathy tone it always did when she felt ill at ease. Right now, Ben's nearness created an unwelcome awkwardness.

He set the box aside and then looked down at his hands as she gathered up the shirts and pants. "I guess I shouldn't pick up any of your clothes."

"I don't need any help. It's okay." Thankfully most of the items were innocent. Shirts. Pants. A dress or two.

Then Ben retrieved the clear garment bag that had lain in the bottom of the box.

"At least this one is protected from my hands," he said.

The heavy plastic crinkled as he raised it up from the sidewalk, a frown creasing his forehead as he looked it over.

Folds of white satin, trimmed with lace, shone and shimmered behind the plastic.

"Is this…" His sentence faded away as he held it up.

"My wedding dress," she finished for him, trying not to cringe at the concrete evidence of the broken places of her life, reflecting the afternoon sun.

"Why do you still have it?"

Shannon sat back on her heels, dredging up the anger she'd clung to after Ben had delivered his horrible news a scant year ago. "I keep it as a reminder."

A reminder of the perfidy of men. A reminder to guard her heart.

Ben carefully laid the bag over his arm, thankfully asking no more questions. Then he caught the handles of the bags she had dropped, picked up another of her boxes and tucked it under his arm. "I imagine you want this brought to the house" was all he said.

"Yes, thank you," she said, gathering up the remainder of the clothes and bags on the sidewalk.

He stepped aside and she led the way to the house. Nana was still upstairs in her room when Shannon pushed the door open with her hip.

Nana stood with her back to the window, a serene smile on her face as she looked past Shannon to Ben. "You are so considerate to help my granddaughter," she said, her tone bordering on effusive. "How lucky you were around when she needed you."

Shannon shot her nana a puzzled glance. What was with her? She sounded positively giddy.

"I was glad to do it." Ben turned to Shannon. "Where do you want this stuff?"

"Just put it on the floor."

Ben did as he was told, but the wedding dress he carefully stretched out on the bed.

"What is that?" Nana asked, shooting Shannon a frown.

Shannon didn't bother to answer, figuring her grandmother's question was rhetorical. Anyone could see it was a wedding dress. Shannon grabbed the box Ben still had tucked under his arm and gave him a quick smile. "Thanks again for your help."

"Anything else you need ferried?" Ben said, slipping his hands in the back pockets of his blue jeans.

"No. I've got it all. Thanks again." His overpowering presence in her bedroom created an unwelcome discomfort and a hint of her previous attraction to him.

Not happening.

"Would you like a cup of lemonade for your troubles?" Nana was asking.

"I don't want to bother you," Ben said.

"It's no bother," Nana replied, taking his arm. "You really should join us and I won't take no for an answer."

"Well, I guess I could have a glass," Ben said, and Shannon's heart sank. She really didn't want to spend social time around a man who made her feel so ill at ease. Especially after he'd seen her old wedding dress.

He probably thought she still pined for the man who had turned her down when, in reality, the unused dress was simply a cautious reminder of what could happen when you let a man get too close.

"Excellent. I'll go get the cups out," Nana said, glancing over her shoulder at Shannon and giving her a broad wink.

As Nana left the room, Shannon thought of her grandmother hurrying her to unload her car. Nana was up to something and Shannon guessed that something involved Ben Brouwer.

Not happening. Not with the brother of her ex-fiancé.

Not with any man, period.

But she couldn't do anything about it for now so she followed her nana downstairs and set out the cups still packed in newspaper, while Nana got together a plate of cookies Hailey had baked as a housewarming gift.

"We still have a few things to unpack," Nana

said with an apologetic smile as she put the plate of cookies on a wooden table, its matching chairs grouped haphazardly around it.

"You've made it look homey already," Ben said, standing by the table while Shannon poured lemonade into the glasses.

He didn't sit down until Nana and Shannon took their seats, earning an approving smile from Nana.

Shannon wasn't as approving. He had ended up only a few inches from her and as he reached to take a cookie from the plate, his arm brushed hers.

Don't jump. Don't react. He's just a guy.

"And you've been making a big difference in your mother's yard," Nana said. "It's looking much more civilized."

"It was a bit overgrown," Ben agreed. "I've been wanting to get at it for some time now."

"Well, it's wonderful you could take time away from your busy work. How is your mother doing?"

As Ben responded to Nana's gentle questioning, he glanced over at Shannon. She managed a lukewarm grin, struggling not to tap her fingers against the table. Nana may have been having fun, but Shannon was growing increasingly uncomfortable sitting so close to Ben. It bothered her more than she cared to admit that he had seen her old wedding dress. It was as if its very presence branded her a loser.

And now he sat in their kitchen sharing lemonade and cookies as if he were a part of the family, sending her the occasional glance as if including her in the two-sided discussion.

"So what do you do in Ottawa?" Nana asked, extending the conversation past its natural life. Nana knew exactly what Ben did. Shannon had explained it all to her when she and Arthur were dating.

"You know he's an E.R. doctor," Shannon said.

"*Was* an E.R. doctor," Ben corrected, then took a final drink of his lemonade and set the empty glass on the table with a *thunk* of finality.

"What do you mean, was?" Nana asked. "Don't you do that anymore?"

Ben slid the empty glass from hand to hand, one side of his lower lip caught between his teeth. "I'm taking a break right now" was all he said.

Shannon caught his gaze and when she saw the desolation in his eyes, she knew she hadn't imagined the cool note in his voice when he responded to Nana's question.

What had happened to him that he needed this break? From what she saw in his expression she sensed it was more than stress.

She held his gaze, her puzzlement growing. Then, to her dismay, she felt it again. That faint trickle of awareness fingering her spine followed by the sensation of attraction she hadn't felt in a long time.

For the tiniest moment she wanted to allow it to grow. To allow that little trill of anticipation, the kind she hadn't felt since Arthur, to begin.

And look where that got you.

Her practical self intervened, thankfully, and quashed her utter foolishness. Getting involved with any guy was silly and futile, especially someone as closely connected to Arthur as Ben was.

"I should get back to work," he said suddenly, pushing his chair away from the table and grabbing his empty glass. "Thanks for the lemonade," he said, giving Nana a polite smile.

Shannon picked up her own glass and got up at the same time, also eager to leave this domestic scene. But as she did, his arm brushed hers.

She couldn't help it. She jumped and dropped her glass.

The cup shattered on the ceramic tiles of the kitchen floor, sending shards of glass skittering across the floor and splashing lemonade all over Ben's blue jeans.

"I'm so sorry," she said, wishing she didn't sound so breathless.

She gathered up the pieces of glass with jerky movements, too aware of Ben now kneeling beside her.

"I'll get a dustpan," Nana announced, her chair screeching across the tiles.

Shannon bit her lip in frustration. What was wrong with her? Why couldn't she act normal around this guy?

"Be careful," Ben warned as Shannon reached under the table to retrieve some more particles.

But he was too late. As she reached, she lost her balance, and fell. A large shard of glass stabbed her knee, sending a flash of pain up her leg.

She flailed her hand, trying to catch her balance, afraid she would cut herself again. Then Ben caught her, his arms holding her steady.

"Are you okay?" he asked, frowning as he looked down at her knee.

No, she wasn't, Shannon thought, looking down at the piece of glass embedded in her knee and the blood flowing freely down her leg, soaking into her pants.

Again their eyes met and locked, but now she was also aware of the warmth of his hands on her arms.

He released her, then pulled out a jackknife from a small leather pouch on his belt. He flipped it open and, with one quick movement, cut her cotton capris away from her leg up to her knee.

She stifled her automatic protest, knowing the bloodstains would probably not wash out of the pants anyway.

"My goodness, what happened?" Nana called out, returning with a dustpan.

My day is complete, Shannon thought.

"Your granddaughter cut herself on some glass," Ben said in a voice that held a note of authority. "I'll need to take her to the hospital." He glanced up at Nana. "She'll need stitches."

Nana slapped her hand to her chest, her face suddenly pale. "Oh, my. What are we going to do? I don't know if I dare drive. I don't know if I can take her."

Ben held up his hand. "Don't worry, Mrs. Beck. I'll take care of getting her there."

"Oh, my," her grandmother muttered again. "That would be nice. Thank you."

"Could you get me a cloth so I can wrap this?" he said to Nana.

"Yes. Of course." Nana grabbed a clean tea towel out of a nearby box and handed it to him.

As Ben wrapped the bleeding wound, his movements were quick, efficient and yet, at the same time, gentle.

He glanced up at her, then pushed himself to

his feet. "Shall we go?" he said, extending his arm to help her.

Shannon would have preferred to walk out on her own steam, but she knew with the glass still embedded in the wound, she would make the bleeding worse if she put too much weight on it.

So she laid her arm on his, wincing as she got to her feet. A new gush of blood stained the tea towel and then, before she could protest, Ben swung her up in his arms.

"Please, I can walk," she said, hating the breathless tone of her voice.

"Better if you don't," he said, shifting her weight in his arms. He looked down at her just as she glanced up.

His dark eyes on hers and his arms holding her close combined to create a flush of awareness both stirring and unwelcome.

"I'll get the door," Nana said, hurrying ahead of them.

As he strode down the hallway, Shannon hesitantly put her arm over his shoulders to brace herself, hoping he didn't notice the blush warming her neck and cheeks.

It was hard being on this side of the curtain.

Ben sat in the waiting room of Hartley Creek Hospital, tapping his thumbs together, forcing himself to stay parked in the leatherette chair.

He heard muffled voices behind the curtain surrounding the bed Shannon lay on. He heard a laugh, which annoyed him.

What could possibly be funny about a two-inch gash across the patella? He doubted the lateral collateral ligament was severed or even nicked, but the cut would require, in his estimation, about ten stitches, maybe fifteen if the doctor had to do a two-layer closure. Personally, on a knee he preferred the two layer.

He caught himself mid-diagnosis. He wasn't here as a doctor. He was simply Shannon's driver.

Old habits, he thought, then laughed at himself. Not that old. Just three months ago he had still been working in a hospital. Still making snap diagnoses, quick calls on what he had to do. When they came into the hospital, the scent of disinfectant had created a sense of anticipation but immediately after had come the regret.

If only he had paid more attention to Saskia, she might still be alive.

And then what? You'd still be divorced.

But he might still be working.

The unwelcome memories pushed him to his feet. He paced down the polished hallway to the end, turned and came back again, glancing at the curtained-off bay in the emergency ward. Shouldn't they be done by now?

He felt the too-familiar clench of dread deep in the pit of his stomach and the unshakeable feeling something bad was going to happen.

At one time he had been a praying man. When these moments of unreasoning fear came over him while he worked, he would try to release them to God. To put himself in God's hands and simply be faithful with what had been given him at the moment.

But he'd seen too much. Lost too much to trust that God would take care of things anymore.

He clenched his fists and forced himself to breathe. It's just a cut that needed stitches. One of the most basic procedures in a busy E.R.

"She'll be fine," the receptionist at the desk said with an indulgent smile, misinterpreting his tension. "Shannon is a tough cookie. You don't have to worry about her."

Ben gave her a curt nod of acknowledgement and turned away from her curious stare. He was sure in a hospital like the one in Hartley Creek most everyone knew most everything about each other. He was also sure this woman was wondering about his connection to Shannon.

He wanted to assure her there was none but kept his comments to himself. He was afraid that anything he said would be taken as either a protest or a cover-up. Arthur had told him enough about Hartley Creek that he understood small-town politics and relationships.

"Ben."

He whirled around at the sound of his name, relief flooding through him when he saw Shannon standing by the desk, a pair of crutches fitted under her arm, her cheeks flushed and her eyes bright. She still wore the capri pants with one leg cut neatly above her bandaged knee.

She caught the direction of his glance and grinned. "Someone finished what you started," she said.

"So I guess you won't be coming in to work tonight?" the nurse beside Shannon asked.

Shannon gave her an apologetic look. "Sorry, Daphne. I wish I could, but Doctor Henneson said I better take it easy for a couple of days so the stitches don't tear loose."

Daphne simply nodded, glancing over at Ben again as if trying to puzzle out where he fit in the picture. "Well, she's all yours for the next few days, Mr. Brouwer. Take good care of her." Then, with a wink Shannon's way, Daphne hurried back behind the curtain separating the emergency department from the main entrance of the hospital.

Ben didn't want to speculate what Daphne's exaggerated wink had been about. "How does your knee feel?" he asked, glancing down at the dressing covering Shannon's wound.

"It throbs a bit. Once the freezing wears off I'm sure I'll feel it more."

"Do you need to get any prescriptions filled?" he asked as she turned and began stumping away from him, her crutches beating out a steady rhythm on the polished floor as she headed toward the entrance.

"No. The cut was clean and because it was glass—"

"I imagine your tetanus shots are up to date."

"Of course."

"You might want to take something for the pain when you get home."

Shannon slowed down, giving him a bemused look. "Are you being a doctor?"

Ben frowned. "No."

"Because it sure sounds like you are," she said, her mouth curving in a curious, off-center smile.

He couldn't help return her smile. "I guess I am. Just a bit," he admitted with a flick of his hand. "I just want to make sure you're okay."

"Dr. Henneson, like the other doctors here, may be overworked, but he's really good at what he does," Shannon said, pausing as the doors leading out of the hospital swung open.

A young woman, heavily pregnant, came

through the doors. Her short dark hair accentuated her pixielike features. Her eyes looked huge in her pale face.

"Hey, Mia," Shannon said. "You okay?"

"Actually, I'm in labor," Mia returned in a breezy voice at odds with what she just told Shannon. "What happened to you?"

Ben glanced at her stomach. From the size of her abdomen and the way she carried, he guessed twins.

"It's nothing. Just a cut that needed stitches. Hey, aren't you early?" Shannon asked, laying a sympathetic hand on her shoulder.

"Yeah, but that's to be expected with twins."

Bingo, Ben thought with a beat of satisfaction. Then Mia took a slow, deep breath.

"Do you need a hand?" Ben couldn't help asking.

She waved off his offer. "I'm okay. This is my third pregnancy. Old hat for me. I'm not that far along yet anyway. Dr. Shuster told me to come in when I felt the first contraction."

"Where's Denton?" Shannon asked, looking behind her for Mia's husband.

"That's the question, isn't it?" Mia said, her voice surprisingly sharp. She sucked in another breath through clenched teeth, then relaxed. "I'm going solo on this one," she said when she had her breath again.

Ben frowned as he watched the exchange. "Seems to me like things are moving along for you. You might want to get going."

A droll grin passed over the woman's mouth. "Thanks for the concern—" She paused, glancing at Shannon with raised eyebrows.

"Ben, this is Mia Strombitsky, ach, I mean Verbeek," Shannon said, still stumbling over Mia's married name.

Mia gave Shannon a bemused look. "I've been married for six years and you still call me by my maiden name?"

Shannon laughed. "I've known you as Strombitsky longer than Verbeek. Anyhow, this is Ben. Ben Brouwer." Shannon stopped there and Mia twitched out a smile, more forced than her previous, candid one.

"I see" was all Mia said.

Ben guessed Mia had realized he was the brother of the man who had left Shannon at the altar.

Then Mia winced again.

"Please, go get yourself admitted," Ben said, wishing this woman would get herself taken care of.

"If I'm in labor, which I doubt I am, it'll be at least half a day yet before these babies come," Mia said with a shrug and another slow intake of breath. "If they are anything like my other kids."

Ben doubted that. If the timing between her breaths was any indication, her contractions were closer than she thought.

"But if it makes you feel any better, I'll head over to the desk." She gave Shannon another quick smile. "You take care of yourself, hear?"

Ben would have had to be deaf to miss the warning tone in Mia's voice and blind to miss the warning glance she shot his way.

You don't have to worry about me, he wanted to tell her as he walked to the door to hold it open for Shannon. *The last thing I want to do is get myself and my emotions tangled up with another woman. Especially my brother's ex-fiancée.*

Chapter Three

Shannon pulled her car up in front of her grandmother's house, turned off the engine and glanced over at Sophie Brouwer kneeling beside an overgrown flower bed at the edge of her property.

Since Arthur had broken up with her, Shannon had managed to avoid any face-to-face meetings with Mrs. Brouwer. From time to time, Shannon had seen Sophie across the street or caught a glimpse of her at some town event. But because Sophie went to a different church and lived on the opposite side of town from where Shannon had, their paths seldom crossed.

Even after she moved into the house, Shannon hadn't seen or talked to Sophie.

Until now.

Shannon turned her car off and eased out of the driver's seat, wincing as she did so. Her knee still throbbed and she was disappointed at her limited mobility. Dr. Henneson had told her she should wait at least four days before returning to work, which didn't exactly put a smile on her face. This meant she only had a couple more shifts before Emma's wedding and, then, getting ready to move to Chicago.

The thought sent a shiver of confused dread through her. Was she ready? Should she go? She would be leaving everything she knew behind and moving to an unfamiliar place and a new job situation.

But what was the alternative? Stay in Hartley Creek for the rest of her life and turn into some spinster who would take her nephews and nieces out because she didn't have any kids of her own?

She banished those happy-happy, joy-joy thoughts, dug her crutches out from the backseat, then stumped around to the passenger side of the car.

"Well, hello, Shannon. Nice to see you. How are you doing, my dear?" Sophie Brouwer asked, looking up from the bright yellow lilies she was rescuing from a mat of chickweed. "Ben said you got a nasty cut on your knee."

Shannon gave Mrs. Brouwer a polite smile as she opened the passenger door of the car and pulled the grocery bags out. "I'm doing okay" was her quiet response.

"And your grandmother? She's well, too?"

Shannon juggled the bags and her handhold on the crutches. "My grandmother is fine, too."

The heavy silence following that scintillating exchange was broken by the thunk of the car door getting pushed shut by Shannon.

"Oh, my goodness, let me help you with those bags." Sophie jumped to her feet and bustled over, brushing her hands on her purple velour jogging pants. "You shouldn't have to carry that by yourself."

"I'm okay. I can manage," Shannon protested.

"I insist," Sophie said, reaching for the bags.

To refuse would not only look ungracious, but, it seemed, would also require a tussle over the plastic bag holding Nana's almond milk and quinoa. And Shannon had enough of spills and accidents happening around members of the Brouwer family.

So she relinquished her hold. Sophie took them but stayed standing directly in front of Shannon, her blue eyes glinting in the bright sunlight.

"And how has work been going for you?" Sophie asked, then shook her head as she looked down at the bandage on Shannon's knee. "Silly me. Of course you haven't been working because of your knee. I know how much you love your job, so I suppose it's hard for you. Right now. Not being able to do your job."

"It is. A bit," Shannon said, adjusting her crutches. She really didn't want to chat with Sophie Brouwer. What could she possibly have to say to her? But to get to the house meant going around Sophie on the grass or pushing past her on the sidewalk, and both would be rude.

"So, we're neighbors now. Never thought that would happen," Sophie was saying. "Though, of course, it was inevitable we bump into each other from time to time." She granted Shannon another simpering smile. "I suppose you are wondering how Arthur is doing?"

Arthur was so far off her radar he may as well have been at the top of Mount Kilimanjaro.

"Last I heard he was working in a car dealership in Fort McMurray," she said. "I understand he really liked the job."

Sophie frowned. "So you've been in contact with him?" She sounded disappointed, which created a flicker of annoyance in Shannon.

"I just heard through the Mug Shots messaging service," she said, trying to reassure Mrs. Brouwer that she didn't have designs on her precious son.

This netted Shannon another frown. Obviously Sophie hadn't caught on to that particular Hartley Creek colloquialism.

"It's what we call any information that gets passed around Mug Shots," Shannon said. "You know. The coffee shop off Main Street. It's a gathering place and people like to chat there. Or gossip, depending on your preference."

Shannon clamped her lips together, blaming the sudden spill of information on her discomfort around Sophie.

"I've been to Mug Shots," Sophie mused. "Wonderful brownies there, though my favorite is the banana bread."

Then the sound of a diesel truck broke into the afternoon quiet. Sophie brightened, glancing from Shannon to the truck. "Look at that. Ben is here," she said with an enthusiasm most people reserve for the arrival of movie stars or royalty.

And right at that instant Nana popped out of the door of the house. "Shannon. I didn't know you were back," she said with a note of glee in her voice. "Oh, look, and there is just the man I need to talk to," she said as she hurried down the walk, waving at Ben, who was getting out of his truck.

"This is perfect," Sophie exclaimed as Nana joined them. "Oh, Eloise. Didn't you say you needed to talk to Ben?"

Shannon shot a puzzled glance from Sophie to her nana. Was it just her or were things getting weird around here?

"Talk to me about what?" Ben said as he pulled a few pieces of lumber out of his truck box. He wore a plaid shirt and blue jeans that held a coating of sawdust. As if he'd been cutting wood all morning.

"Well, you know how you said you can't do anything more on the yard until that lawn edging you ordered comes in?" Sophie was saying, turning to her son, who brought the lumber to the sidewalk and laid it down. "And I know how you like to keep busy and Mrs. Beck has found a couple of holes in the wall of her house and—" here she looked back at Nana as if confirming her information "—didn't you say something about a cabinet coming off the wall?"

"In the kitchen." Nana shot Shannon a petulant look. "I found it this morning. The one I had all the dishes in. Almost had the whole cupboard fall down. Luckily I saw it and emptied it. It really needs to get fixed. That real-estate agent wasn't forthcoming about the problems in the house."

And you were in such a rush to move in you weren't asking many questions, Shannon wanted to say.

"So Eloise was telling me about her problems and I told her you are handy with a hammer." Here Sophie took a moment to look from Ben to Shannon. "He put himself through university working as a carpenter."

Shannon felt like Alice in Wonderland tumbling down the rabbit hole, trying to find which way was up or down. She dared a look at Ben who seemed as dumbfounded as she was.

"Anyhow—" Nana dragged the word out as if to signify to Sophie to move the conversation along "—Sophie mentioned Ben might be able to help us out in the house." Here she gave Ben a gracious smile. "That is, if you are willing to do so."

Ben's frown wasn't encouraging, but, undaunted, Sophie plunged in. "This would really help out Mrs. Beck," she said to her son. "And I don't mind if you take some time away from working on the yard. Like I said, you can't do much until the edging comes in."

"I don't know if I can help," he said, reluctance lacing his voice. "I haven't done much carpentry work in a while."

"And doctors shouldn't be using hammers and nails anyway," Shannon put in. She shot Ben a quick glance and caught him looking at her. For a few seconds she couldn't look away and, to be honest, didn't want to.

Then she checked herself and pulled her gaze free. Having Arthur's brother underfoot was not a good idea.

"It would really help me out," Nana was saying in her most convincing voice. "I would so appreciate it."

"And this way you won't be bored," Sophie added.

Silence followed her suggestion and Shannon sensed that Ben was as reluctant to work in the house as she was to have him there.

"Couldn't you hire someone?" Shannon asked her nana, hoping to give the guy an out.

"I've been on the phone for the past half hour. All the contractors in town are busy." Nana lifted her hands in a "what can I do?" gesture.

Shannon tried to catch her grandmother's gaze, but Nana had her eyes firmly fixed on Ben.

"I suppose I could have a look at it," Ben said. "See what I could do."

"That would be perfect." Nana turned to Shannon and it wasn't hard to catch the triumph in her expression. "Isn't that good of Ben to help us out, Shannon?"

Shannon could only hope her smile held at least a modicum of sincerity. "Yeah. Awesome." She stole a glance Ben's way, surprised, again, to see him watching her.

And even more surprised and dismayed to feel that spark of attraction.

She closed her eyes and clenched her fists.

Stay focused, she reminded herself. *You're only here until after the wedding. Then you're gone.*

She couldn't afford the distraction of any man. Least of all a man like Ben Brouwer.

One of these days he would learn to say no, Ben thought as he moved the stepladder into the living room to tackle the second hole in Eloise Beck's house.

Ben didn't want to be angry with his mother for putting him on the spot yesterday, but he certainly felt frustrated with her manipulation.

As a result he was now pulling down drywall in Mrs. Beck's house and Shannon was cleaning up. Somehow Mrs. Beck had found some errands to run, which meant he and Shannon had been alone for the past two hours. And for the past two hours he'd been aware of her every movement.

Ben pushed down a sigh, centered his metal ruler on the stud beside the gaping hole and ran his utility knife along the ruler. He cut again to get all the way through, then tugged at the ragged pieces of drywall, dropping them onto the floor. He had tried cleaning them up himself, but Shannon was always right there, gathering and sweeping.

"Hello, house," a woman's bright voice called

out from the hallway. That wasn't Mrs. Beck, Ben thought as the front door slammed shut.

"Well, I suppose this is a start," the same cheery voice announced.

Ben looked over at the young woman standing in the doorway of the front room, a plate of cupcakes in one hand and a thermos in the other, her olive-green T-shirt setting off the copper of her hair and accenting the green of her eyes.

"Hailey. What brings you to town?" Shannon asked, slowly getting up from the floor, brushing the dust out of her hair. She had pulled it back into a ponytail that hung over one shoulder. The pink shirt she wore was also covered in dust and her cheek held a black smudge that had come from who knows where.

And she still managed to look amazing.

"I come bearing gifts," Hailey said, holding aloft her plate and the thermos. "And I come with plans."

"For what?" Shannon asked, slowly stretching out her knee as though it bothered her. Ben hadn't wanted her to help, but she had insisted, saying she would go crazy sitting around. Trouble was, she was turning out to be more of a distraction than a help.

"Let's have some coffee and I can tell you." Hailey shot a quick glance Ben's way. "So, this is really generous of you to help my grandmother," she said, her eyes taking on a mischievous glint.

He wasn't sure what to say to that. *Generous* didn't really describe how he felt about this. *Railroaded* would be a better word.

"I live to serve" was all he said.

This was greeted with a chuckle by Hailey. "Awesome. I'm sure Shannon could use some more of your serving unpacking her boxes when you're done here."

"Why don't we just mosey on to the kitchen and we can eat those cupcakes that are making my mouth water?" Shannon suggested.

"I'm almost done here, then I can get the dry-wall I need to cover the holes," Ben said, hoping the sisters would get the hint. He didn't really want to sit in the kitchen with Shannon. "I'd like to get done here."

He'd come here to retreat from problems and live a simple life for a while. Do ordinary things in a nonthreatening environment. Having to spend this much time with Shannon was an emotional complication he didn't want encumbering his life.

And yet—

"Plenty of time to get the work done," Hailey assured him. "I'm sure Nana doesn't mind if you take a break. Besides, I think Shannon should be putting her foot up for a while."

Well, there is that, he conceded.

A few minutes later he was again sitting a little too close to Shannon, drinking tea and eating some ridiculously good cupcakes.

"These are delicious," he said, then took another bite.

"Shannon's recipe," Hailey said, resting her elbows on Mrs. Beck's minuscule table. "She's an awesome cook. You should get her to make you supper sometime."

Shannon gave her sister a suspicious look, then rotated her hand. "Plans? Spill?"

"So very bossy," Hailey said, rolling her eyes. "Emma wants us all to come to the ranch tomorrow, for a barbecue. You're not working for a couple of days, so this time you can come." Then Hailey gave him a quick smile, including him in her conversation. "And because you *have* been working—on my grandmother's house, that is—we'd like you to come, too."

"I've hardly done enough—"

"You will have by tomorrow night," Hailey assured him with a grin. Then she frowned. "Why are you kicking me?" she asked her sister.

Probably for the same reason he felt suddenly awkward at the invitation and even being around Hailey herself.

The last time he'd seen Hailey was when he delivered Arthur's "news." She had been helping

Shannon with her wedding dress and the look she had given him was far less kindly than the look he was getting from her now.

"I'm not sure that's a good idea," Ben was saying, shifting himself away from the invite.

Hailey glanced from Shannon to Ben, her clasped hands resting on the table as if she was about to deliver some important pronouncement. "I know the last time we were all together was under less than ideal circumstances," she said in a matter-of-fact voice.

"He came to tell me that my wedding was canceled." Shannon's voice held a note of bitterness that made Ben feel, again, like the biggest heel in the history of heels. "'Less than ideal' hardly covers it."

"Okay, rotten, then," Hailey conceded, putting her hand over her sister's.

"Really rotten."

"But it wasn't his fault and he's living next door and I am sure he doesn't know anybody—"

"And he's right here," Ben said, leaning back in his chair trying to gain some control of this conversation. "And not deaf."

Shannon's mouth tweaked up in a smile as she looked over his way.

"Sorry about that." Then she eased out a sigh as if unsure of where to go from here.

Ben looked from Hailey to Shannon, wishing he knew what to say or how to change what had happened. But now that it was on the table, this was his chance to at least make some part of that afternoon right.

"Just for the record, I didn't want to be the one to tell you," he said quietly, his gaze meshing with hers. "I said I was sorry then. I know it's too small a word, but it's the only one I have at my disposal. If it's any consolation, I think you're better off without my brother."

Shannon laid her finger across her lips as if contemplating what he was saying. Then a slow smile drifted across her mouth. "Arthur always said he admired your ability to tell the truth. So, I'll take what you're saying at face value."

"For what that's worth," Ben replied.

"More than you might think."

All that could be heard in the silence following her statement was the steady tick of the clock above the table behind them.

As their gazes held for a few more beats, Ben felt as if a load he hadn't even been aware he carried had dropped off his shoulders.

And once again, he couldn't look away.

"So. Now that we have that cleared up," Hailey said, her voice tearing the fabric of the moment. "Are you coming to the barbecue, Ben?"

He dragged his reluctant attention back to

Hailey and responded with a vague shrug. "Not sure. I don't want to leave my mother alone."

"I think her and Nana are going to some book-club meeting at the Book Nook that night," Hailey said.

"But Nana loves coming out to the ranch." Shannon frowned in puzzlement. "Why would she sooner go to a book-club meeting?"

Hailey lifted her hands in a gesture of confusion. "Don't ask me. I only know she said something about not getting in the way of the plans. Whatever that might be." Then she gave Ben a quick smile. "But I sure hope you can come out. The ranch is beautiful this time of the year."

Ben wavered. On the one hand, sitting in his mother's house all alone on a Saturday night held the faintest whiff of loser.

But to spend time with Shannon's family and spend social time with Shannon herself?

"I'll think about it" was all he said, though, if he was honest, the idea held some appeal.

"Okay. That's where we'll leave it then." Hailey picked up the plate. "But at least have another cupcake and if you come to the ranch, there's more where these came from."

"You look lovely," Nana Beck said in an approving voice. "I especially like your hair like that."

Shannon's hand crept to the flowered clip she had, at the last minute, put in her hair. Just for fun, she'd told herself. It had nothing to do with Ben.

Because he wasn't coming.

"Thanks, Nana." Shannon glanced at the book bag her grandmother had hanging over her arm. "So tell me again why you're going to this book-club thingy and not coming out to the barbecue at the ranch?"

Nana flapped her hand at Shannon in a gesture of dismissal. "Oh, I thought it would be nice for you kids to get together without me. Sophie said she wanted to go to the meeting but not by herself so I thought we could do it together."

"And since when did you and Sophie become such fast friends?" Shannon asked. "A year ago you practically blew a blood vessel every time someone mentioned Arthur's name and now you're going to book club with his mother?"

"It wasn't her fault Arthur was so irresponsible. In fact she told me she feels really badly about it. She would like to tell you, as well, but doesn't think you would want to hear it from her."

Shannon's mind slipped back to the conversation she, Ben and Hailey had had yesterday. Curiously, Ben's concern and apology had mitigated some of the pain she had carried around too long. And when he had said that she was better off without Arthur, part of her had wanted to cling to those words, fold them up and store them away for the times when self-pity dug its spiteful claws into her.

"You can tell her I've moved on, so she doesn't have to worry."

Nana lifted one questioning eyebrow. "Really?"

"Yes. Really," she said with more conviction than she felt. She knew her nana was obliquely referring to the dress still hanging in her bedroom cupboard.

"That's good then." Nana smoothed a strand of hair away from her forehead, then gave Shannon a quick smile. "You kids have fun tonight and tell my grandchildren that when this house is shipshape, we'll have a get-together here."

"I will."

Nana bent over and brushed a kiss over her forehead. "I love you, my dear. Never forget that." She straightened and touched her finger to the gold nugget Shannon wore around her neck. "And I want you to remember, as I told you when I gave you this and the Bible, that God's love is more faithful than anyone's."

Warmth seeped into Shannon's soul. She smiled back at her nana, thinking of the Bible she had, still packed away in a box in her room, knowing she should take it out and read it again. "I won't forget."

"That's good." Then Nana frowned as Shannon pulled her coat out of the closet just off the entrance. "Is that what you're wearing tonight?"

Shannon looked down at the brightly colored plaid shirt she wore over her blue jeans. "Yeah."

"But...I thought... Shouldn't you dress up a bit?"

Shannon frowned at her nana. "It's just a barbecue."

"But isn't Ben coming? Sophie said he was."

Shannon's frown deepened. "He never said anything about coming when he left this afternoon. To be honest, I kind of hope he doesn't."

Really? Then why did it take you so long to pick out your clothes? And why did you tuck that flower in your hair?

Nana looked taken aback at her blunt reply. "Why ever not?"

"Seriously, Nana? He's the one who came to my house to tell me Arthur didn't want to marry me. Hardly a good lasting impression."

Nana looked genuinely puzzled. "That wasn't his fault," she protested.

And Ben had apologized about that, but still...

"He's Arthur's brother. It's weird even being around him. He's the last person I would want to spend more time with." Shannon spoke the words with more conviction than she felt.

Trouble was, after spending a couple of days with Ben, her resistance to him was shifting and changing and she didn't like being in that position with him or any man.

Nana sighed. "Please don't talk like that. I don't want to see you turn into a bitter old woman because of what Arthur did to you. I remember you saying to Hailey, when she struggled with what to do about Dan, that there are other fish in the sea."

"But I'm not fishing, Nana," Shannon said.

Nana sighed as if giving in and patted Shannon's cheek. "You know I pray for you every day and I still pray that someone may come into your life who will show you that not all men are like Arthur."

A knock on the door broke into their conversation. And when Nana opened the door, Ben Brouwer stood on the step. His chin was smooth and free of his usual stubble. His hair was brushed and he wore a clean shirt and blue jeans.

And in spite of her protests only a moment ago, Shannon's heart did a gentle flop.

"I was wondering if you're still going to the barbecue," he asked, glancing from Nana to

Shannon. "Your grandmother said you might need a ride."

Shannon fought back the hope rising up in her chest. What was wrong with her? Hadn't she just told Nana she wasn't interested in this guy?

Then what he said registered.

"I don't think I need a ride—"

Nana put her hand on Shannon's shoulder. "I forgot to tell you, but there's something wrong with my car and I was hoping to use yours. So having Ben drive you to the ranch would make it easier for me to go to the book club."

Shannon felt confused as she looked from Ben to her grandmother. "But why don't I drive you—"

"I don't want you to rush home from the ranch to pick me up. This is the easiest solution." Then her nana flashed Ben a grateful smile. "Thanks so much for doing me this favor. Shannon hates missing out on family gatherings."

Then with another wave and a jingle of Shannon's car keys, her nana glided out the door, her smile serene.

Ben gave Shannon an apologetic smile as they walked out of the house together. "Sorry about that. I thought she told you."

"No, I had no clue what was going on," she said, looking past Ben as Sophie joined her nana by Shannon's car.

Then, just before they got into the car, they both looked over at Shannon and Ben, now standing on the veranda of the house. When Shannon caught the smug look on her nana's face she knew there was nothing wrong with Nana's car. That had been some ruse concocted by her grandmother to get Ben to drive Shannon to the ranch.

Her back stiffened at her nana's matchmaking machinations.

No way, no how, she thought, not even looking over at Ben as she walked toward his truck. *No matter how much finagling Nana does, Ben is a complication I can't allow in my life.*

Chapter Four

"Did Garret say when he was coming back?" Hailey asked as she finished wiping off the large kitchen table.

Dinner was over at Emma and Carter's home and everyone seemed to know what they were supposed to do except Ben. He had offered to help, but had been waved off and told he was company and to just sit.

"He said he'd be here to stand up for me at the wedding," Carter replied, drying the last large pot that couldn't fit in the dishwasher. "But he said he couldn't stick around and had to head out early the next morning. Gave me some song and dance about big plans afoot."

"Was that plan G or H?" Shannon asked with a laugh, taking the pot from Carter and putting it in the cupboard.

"Probably K. I can't keep up with the guy."

Ben sat back in his chair in one corner of the kitchen listening to the lively banter in the farmhouse where Emma and her son lived. So far he had discovered that Carter and Emma were getting married in a few weeks and that Carter had an identical twin named Garret who currently worked overseas as a consultant in the oil and gas industry, apparently raking in the money.

There was another cousin, Naomi. Every time her name came up the conversation grew more subdued. Apparently her fiancé was dying of cancer and she was at his bedside in Halifax, clear across the country, taking care of him.

A number of times during dinner, Shannon had apologized to Ben for leaving him out, but Ben didn't mind. He liked listening to the vigorous back and forth of conversation among these family members who had grown up together and had, apparently, spent most of their time on this ranch.

He also didn't mind seeing how Shannon's reserve lowered around her family. Her eyes sparkled and as she talked her delicate hands punctuated her comments. And she laughed a lot more.

"Did you hear how he did on those penny stocks he got that big tip on?" Dan, Hailey's boyfriend and fiancé asked, continuing the conversation.

"If he did well, we'll hear," Carter said, tossing his dish towel in a basket beside the stove. "If he lost money, you won't get that information out of him with a pry bar."

Carter's wry observation netted him a laugh.

"What's a pry bar?" Adam, Emma's little boy, asked as he and Dan's daughter, Natasha, came into the kitchen. Adam was a bright boy of five with the same dark brown eyes and hair as his mother, Emma. Natasha, with her long dark hair, could be his sister but for her strong chin, a tiny replica of her father.

As soon as Carter had finished praying after dinner, the two kids had both bolted out of their chairs and headed to the living room, probably to avoid having to help with the dishes.

But no one seemed to hear Adam's question so he turned to Ben, his brown eyes brightly inquisitive. "Do you know what a pry bar is, Dr. Brouwer?"

"Just Mr. Brouwer." As soon as Ben spoke the words he regretted his sharp tone, and the puzzled look on the boy's face only underlined it.

"But my Auntie Hailey said you were a doctor," Adam replied. "And my mommy always told me I had to call Dr. Henneson 'Doctor.' Why don't you want to be called that?"

The boy's sudden confusion made Ben feel like a heel. He shouldn't have been so touchy. He was about to formulate some kind of response when Shannon came limping toward them.

"Adam, honey, why don't you show me your new colt?" she asked with a bright smile, as if trying to distract the little boy. "Your mom said that she is really pretty."

"I want to come, too," Natasha called out.

"Of course you can," Shannon said, avoiding Ben's expression of gratefulness for her diversion. She took Natasha's hand and walked slowly toward the door leading from the kitchen outside, favoring her sore knee. She shot a quick glance over her shoulder to see if Adam was coming.

But Adam, it seemed, wasn't done with Ben. He turned and grabbed Ben's hand. "Do you want to come with us and see our foal, Dr.—I mean, Mr. Brouwer? She's really pretty."

"I guess..." Ben hesitated, glancing around the kitchen to see if anyone else was coming along, but no one paid much attention to the two of them. And Shannon was already out the door.

"Have you ever seen a foal before?" Adam asked.

"No. I haven't," Ben admitted.

"Then you have to come," Adam said, now tugging on his hand.

He had already caused the boy some discomfort; it would be rude of him not to come along now.

"Of course I'll come. I'd love to see your colt." Ben got to his feet, letting Adam lead him around the table.

"Actually she's a filly, but Carter...my dad... says you can call her a foal, too," Adam said, leading Ben past Carter, Hailey, Dan and Emma, who still lounged around the kitchen counters, discussing Carter and Emma's upcoming wedding and who would do what.

"When she's older, then for sure you have to call her a filly. If she was a boy, you could call her a foal, too, but you would have to call her a colt. If it was a him. I know it's mixed-up, but you'll get used to it."

"Well, then. Thanks for the lesson," Ben said, unable to suppress a grin at the boy's matter-of-fact tone.

"Don't let him talk your ear off," Emma said with a smile as Adam led him to the door leading outside.

"It's okay," Ben said. "I don't mind."

"You say that now," Carter said, playfully flicking his tea towel at Adam. "Wait until he tells you his plans for his tree house."

Adam stopped and turned to Ben. "Do you want to see my tree house, too?"

Carter gave Ben a sheepish look. "Sorry. I shouldn't have given him any ideas."

"You don't need to give that youngster any

ideas," Hailey put in. "He has more than enough to spare."

Ben just laughed, then followed Adam out the door.

Sunshine and warmth washed over them and as they walked across the yard Ben's eyes shifted to the mountains surrounding the ranch. The foothills were carpeted in undulating green that gave way to hard granite, laced with snow higher up their ragged peaks.

On the trip up here Shannon had been surprisingly loquacious, telling him all about the ranch, how it had been in the Beck family for generations. How she and her sisters spent most of their weekends and summers here.

The entire time she talked her face was animated and her eyes sparkled and many times he caught himself unable to look away from her. She was the very epitome of life and vitality, a complete contrast to the reserved persona he had seen since he came to Hartley Creek.

But now, as he gazed at the panorama stretched out before him, he understood her enthusiasm. Everywhere he had gone in Hartley Creek, the mountains had been present, surrounding the town. He sometimes had to remind himself to keep his eyes on the road and stop bending over to catch the sun on the mountains.

Then on the drive here each turn of the roads

snaking along the river valley brought new vistas and views more beautiful than the next until they had arrived here.

"Auntie Shannon, wait for us," Adam called out, pulling Ben toward the red barn ahead of them.

Shannon, limping ahead, holding Natasha's hand, hadn't gotten very far so when she stopped and turned around he easily saw the frown on her face.

But her frown quickly morphed into a polite smile as he came closer. "So you brought a friend," she said to Adam.

"Dr. Brouwer—I mean Mr. Brouwer—has never seen a foal before so I said he had to come."

"Why did you call him Dr. Brouwer?" Natasha put in, obviously not missing Adam's correction.

"Because he's a doctor, but he asked me to not to call him that. He wants me to call him Mr. Brouwer," Adam said.

This netted him another confused look from Natasha.

"So your filly is inside this barn?" Ben asked, forestalling the questions he could see formulating behind Natasha's eyes.

Adam thankfully took the hint and, grasping the handle of the large door, started tugging to pull it open. Ben hurried to help him and together they slid the door aside.

A wave of cool air washed over them as they stepped into the shadowy interior. It smelled like hay blended with the musky scent of horse.

As Ben's eyes adjusted to the weak light he noticed a number of empty stalls along one wall, but a rustling in the far one told him which one held the horse and her baby.

"We have to be quiet," Adam whispered as he led the way. "We don't want to scare Two Bits." He walked slowly to the last stall and stepped up on a bale of hay lying in front of the half-wooden door.

Ben followed Adam and looked into the opening of the stall.

And he was overcome with wonder.

A dark brown mare stood inside, shifting her hooves on the straw bedding of the stall, watching them, nickering softly toward the far corner of the stall where the foal lay.

Her head was up, her dark eyes watching them. Her hide was a golden-brown, and her mane, just a brush of hair along the top of her neck, was jet-black. As they watched, she clambered to her feet, still unsteady on long, ungainly legs.

"Oh, she's so cute," Natasha breathed, clinging to the edge of the door. "Can I go in and pet her?"

"Not yet." Shannon rested her elbows on the door, a gentle smile teasing her lips. "I think the mommy would like it better if we just look for now."

"What are you naming her?" Ben asked, grinning as the colt stumbled toward its mother.

"I want to call it Koocanusa, after the lake, but my mom said that the name is bigger than the filly, so maybe Bolt. Or Flicker."

"How about Flicka?" Shannon said. "Like in the movie *My Friend Flicka.*"

"I like Flicka." Natasha rested her chin on her hands and sighed. "I think she would be fun to ride."

"Carter…my dad…says it will be a long time before we can ride her," Adam said. He leaned back, still hanging on to the edge of the door. "But Dusty is the horse I ride until Flicka is big enough."

The colt stumbled around a bit more; then the mare nudged it closer to her side. But even as Ben watched, his attention was just as much on the woman beside him as the colt in front of him.

She shifted her weight and as her hair brushed his arm he caught the faint scent of her perfume, a flowery scent at odds with the musky smell of the barn. "She's so cute," she murmured, her voice full of awe.

They watched the colt awhile, laughing occasionally as she tried to walk around.

"How old does she have to be before you can ride her?" Ben asked.

"I think Carter figured about two or three, depending on how heavy the person is," Shannon said, resting her chin on her stacked hands.

"Have you gone riding?" Ben asked Shannon.

"Used to all the time when we came here. We used to race each other around the field and often got into trouble with Grandpa for tearing up the hay field. Usually we behaved and rode the trails up the mountains." Her smile transformed her face, putting a sparkle in her eyes, softening her features.

Making her even more attractive than she already was.

As if sensing his regard, her gaze slid toward him, her hazel eyes holding his.

"Sounds like you and your cousins had a lot of fun here."

Her smile grew and with it, her appeal. "Many good memories, that's for sure."

They were quiet again, the only sound the rustling of the new colt's hooves in the straw and a low throated whicker from his mother.

"I'm going to the tree house," Adam announced all of a sudden, jumping down from the stool.

"I'm coming, too," Natasha said, scrambling down from her perch by the door, leaving Ben and Shannon alone.

As if unwilling to be left alone with him, Shannon followed the kids out of the barn, but paused at the door, a wince of pain distorting her face.

"Are you okay?"

Shannon waved off his concern. "I'm fine. My knee just twinges now and again if I put too much weight on it."

"It's not infected, is it? Have you noticed any redness? Swelling?"

Shannon gave him an oblique look. "Are you being a doctor now?"

He shrugged aside her comment. "Just concerned." He saw another bale of hay just inside the door and dragged it outside, pushing it up against the barn. "Here. Sit down. You can watch the kids from here."

"You sure sound like a doctor," Shannon said, but she didn't make any move to sit down.

"And you are acting like every nurse I've ever worked with," he retorted. "Just rest for a few moments. No one will think you're a wimp."

Her laugh ricocheted through his heart and softened her smile. Since coming to the ranch she appeared more relaxed. As if she'd sloughed off her habitual reserve and became this softer, kinder version of Shannon Deacon.

"Okay, Dr. Brouwer." She slid down onto the bale, watching the kids, who were swinging from a pair of old tires attached to a crossbeam of a tree fort.

"Lucky kids," Ben said slipping his hands in the pockets of his blue jeans, leaning against the doorway of the barn. The wood was still warm from the sun, which was now drifting down toward the mountains. In the silence surrounding them he heard the faint nicker of the mare and her colt in the barn behind them, the chirp of some birds as they flew past the barns and the burbling of a creek coming from the woods edging the yard. "Whenever I think of the perfect way to raise a kid, this is the image that comes to mind," he said, releasing a sigh as the peace of the place seemed to ease the relentless grip of tension that had held him since he left Ottawa.

"It comes pretty close to heaven, that's for sure."

Ben looked around and released a cynical laugh. "I'm not so sure I believe in heaven anymore. Or God. And if I did, I would want a few choice words with him."

No sooner had the words left his mouth than he wished he could take them back. Shannon didn't need to know about his faith or lack thereof. She had just been making a general statement, the kind sentimental people make around children and nature. He blamed his response on the effect this place had on him. It made him lower his reserves.

"Did you once believe in God?" Shannon asked.

How was he supposed to get back to ordinary conversation after revealing this much? Besides, he knew that Shannon was a Christian, as was the rest of her family. The conversation around the dinner table had showed him as much, as had the devotions they'd had after dinner was over.

"I did. Once," he admitted. "My mom and dad took us to church and I did all the churchy kind of things. But then life took over and God got pushed to the side."

"I imagine working in the E.R. in a big city didn't help bring God back into the forefront?"

Ben kept his attention on Adam and Natasha and the bits of their indistinct chatter floating back to him and Shannon. Two innocent children he prayed would never see the things he had.

"It's hard to get a real grasp of a loving, caring heavenly father when you see so much death," he finally said with a sigh of resignation.

"But you saw life, too, didn't you?"

He let her comment sift down through his memories and felt the subtle undertow of happier times. The mother of three who had flatlined, then, inexplicably, come back. The baby who had been left to die but refused to. The couple badly injured, but still clinging to each other, unwilling to let go.

He let them drift up to the surface, but then, with them, came the sound of his ex-wife's voice on the telephone. The panic edging her words.

Her pleading for him to come to talk to her. Pleading that he had ignored.

"Ben? Are you okay?" Shannon's words were underlined by her touch. It was no more than the brushing of her fingers over his arm, but he jumped.

He shook his head, as if dislodging the memories, then forced a smile as he pulled himself back to the present.

"I understood from the conversation around the dinner table you and your sisters spent a lot of time out here," he said, determined to shift the topic to the present.

She smiled, her eyes drifting as if gathering up the memories. "Most every weekend and as much of the summer as our mother would allow. Which was usually most of it when we were younger." The faint note of resentment in her voice was at odds with her smile. "Thankfully Nana didn't mind having the place overrun with grandkids all summer. Though I think she was pretty pleased that Grandpa built the cabins later on."

"What cabins?"

"Over there. By the swings the kids are playing on."

Ben followed the direction of her finger and then saw three small log cabins standing in a row tucked between another shed and the tree fort. "I can't believe I didn't see them when we drove up here."

"You were too busy looking at the mountains," she said with a gentle laugh. Her gaze drifted over the yard, then came to rest on him.

"Don't get to see them too much out east." He returned her smile but didn't look away. Her smile wavered, but to his surprise she didn't look away, either.

And for a moment an indefinable emotion hovered between them. He wanted to brush it away, to ignore it, but the loneliness in his soul let the moment linger in spite of who she was and what had happened to him.

Then Shannon blinked and looked back at the children, her hands now resting open on her lap. "I love this place," she said abruptly. "I'll miss it when I move to Chicago."

"What made you choose Chicago?" he asked. He was still surprised she had chosen to work there after living in Hartley Creek.

She shrugged as she twisted a strand of hair around her finger again. "I saw an advertisement for travel nurses and I thought it might be interesting to live in a big city for a change. And the money was good."

"You don't strike me as the kind of person to whom money would be important."

"Guess you don't know that much about me," she said with a humorless laugh.

"I know some. Arthur did talk about you from time to time."

The stricken look she shot him made him want to kick himself for bringing up his brother's name. But then she looked away, her eyes on the children.

"I'm surprised I even rated a mention in any of his conversations," she said, a faint note of bitterness in her voice. "Other than to get you to tell me he didn't want to marry me."

Ben folded his arms over his chest, watching the children playing, trying to find the right way to tell her what he had wanted to since he had delivered that awful news.

"I should never have agreed to deliver that message for him," he said. "But I had to."

Shannon stretched her injured leg in front of

her then pulled in a long breath. "Arthur should have done his own dirty work. You didn't need to do it for him."

"Arthur was gone."

Shannon's eyes shot to his. "What do you mean?"

"When I came to town before the wedding, Arthur had already skipped town. He left me a note."

Her eyes narrowed and he could see her hands clenching in her lap. "Why didn't you tell me that?" The anger in her voice didn't surprise him, but the intensity of it did.

"I don't know why I didn't tell you he'd left. I was too busy wanting to throttle him myself."

Shannon blinked, and to his dismay he saw a glimmer of moisture in her eyes, but then she blinked and it was gone.

"He may be my brother," he continued, "but, as I said before, you deserve better than him."

Shannon's only response was a vague shrug. She looked as if she was about to say more when Adam called out.

"Mr. Brouwer, see how high I'm going?"

"I see," Ben returned, adding a wave in case the boy didn't hear him. "That's pretty amazing."

"Adam seems quite taken with you," Shannon said.

"I guess so" was all he could say, still watching the children playing. "Though I don't know why. I haven't done anything to encourage that." He couldn't help remembering how he had responded to the boy just a few moments ago.

"He's a sweet kid." Shannon leaned back against the wall, her fingers still twirling her hair, though her movements had slowed. "I hope I'm not being presumptuous, but you seemed upset when Adam wanted to address you as Doctor."

He kept his eyes on Adam and Natasha, listening to their carefree laughter and feeling as if Shannon had some kind of key to his inner thoughts.

But he decided to be straightforward.

"Calling me Doctor is way too formal outside of the hospital, that's all. And since I'm not practicing right now—" He caught himself. What was wrong with him? Why did he tell her that?

"I thought you were just taking a break?" Shannon's question came out quietly, but he caught a hint of determination in it.

"I am," he said, hoping he sounded more carefree than he felt, as his mind drifted back to the past.

"Will you be going back to Ottawa when your break is over?"

Her question pulled him back to the present. He blinked, orienting himself, then shook his head. "No. Not a chance."

"So would you go somewhere else?"

He lifted his shoulders in a shrug. He didn't want to look beyond his current job of patching up the holes in the drywall of her grandmother's house and fixing up his mother's yard.

"If I can put in a plug for the hospital here in Hartley Creek," Shannon was saying. "They're short-staffed and desperately looking for a doctor."

He let the comment lie between them. He didn't want to look rude by dismissing it, but he wasn't responding to her employment suggestion. Lately his thoughts and plans weren't moving in that direction.

And where are you going? All your life you wanted to be a doctor. What else would you do?

"Don't think I'm interested," he said.

"Why not?"

"Because being a doctor just…"

To his annoyance he couldn't finish the sentence.

"Just what?" Shannon pressed.

"I should go check on the kids," he said, pushing himself away from the barn without responding to her question.

He knew he was avoiding her and as he walked away, he could feel her eyes following him.

She doesn't need to know anything, he reminded himself. *She's a temporary blip in your life. She's going to Chicago and you're going—*

He clenched his fists as if holding the thoughts in.

Just because I don't have a destination, doesn't mean I'm lost. But as he strode toward the swings and the children, he couldn't shake the feeling that he was.

Nor could he shake the feeling Shannon wasn't letting this go.

"Are you sure you're okay? You look a little pale." Emma slowed her pace as she walked with Shannon down the sidewalk of the house toward Ben's truck.

A burst of laughter floated across the yard, and Shannon glanced past Ben's truck to the corrals where Ben, Carter, Dan, Hailey and the children had gathered, watching the new colt. Carter had let the mare and her filly out of the barn and Shannon suspected the laughter was over the colt's antics.

"My knee is bothering me, that's all," Shannon said.

"You should have Dr. Ben take a look at it,"

Emma said with a grin. "I'm sure he won't mind the opportunity to ease your pain."

"In case you've forgotten, I am a registered nurse and just as capable of making a decision about my knee as he is." Shannon didn't mean for her comment to come out sounding so defensive. Emma had been making a joke.

But since she and Ben had come back from looking at the colt with the kids she had put up with knowing smirks from her sister and raised eyebrows from her future cousin-in-law, Emma.

She'd ignored them all. Saying nothing was usually the best defense around her family. When any of them had a chance, they would do the "wink, wink, nudge, nudge" thing that had become prevalent in the family since Hailey and Carter's engagement.

Emma slipped her hands in the back pockets of her blue jeans, giving Shannon a coy look. "So you and the good doctor—"

"Please. Just stop," Shannon protested.

"He's way better-looking than Arthur," Emma continued as if she hadn't heard her friend. "And then there's that whole doctor-nurse thingy."

Shannon hurried her pace as if to outrun her friend's innuendos. But that was a mistake. Pain stabbed her knee. She stumbled and would have fallen if not for Emma catching her.

"Okay. I'm sorry. I didn't mean to upset you,"

Emma said, helping her regain her balance. "Please forgive me?"

Shannon held Emma's dark eyes and when she saw the contrition in her expression, she relented. "I do. But please, no more talk about Ben."

Emma dropped her head to one side. "Really? Why?"

Didn't she get it?

"He's Arthur's brother, that's why."

"So?"

"It's strange and…bizarre and…" She hesitated, wishing she could articulate her reasons. "Family get-togethers would be more strained what with Arthur and all."

"Still not seeing the problems here," Emma said. "You said yourself you're over Arthur. And he's not even around much. Besides, Ben is a way better catch. And I think he's interested in you. I caught him watching you a lot."

This information did nothing for Shannon's already shaky equilibrium. Spending time with Ben around Carter and Emma, who were full of talk of their upcoming wedding, and Dan and her sister Hailey, who now sported a delicate engagement ring, created an unspoken assumption that now it was Shannon's turn. And why not with the single guy she had come with?

"I'm moving to Chicago." Shannon threw out

the comment like a trump card. "I'm moving on with my life by getting away from this town."

Emma's expression grew dour. "Do you really think that will fix anything?"

"It will fix everything," Shannon said, turning and walking back toward the truck, but a bit more slowly this time. "Every time I turn around in this town I feel as if people don't see me, Shannon Deacon. They see the poor bride that got dumped just before her wedding. The girl who couldn't keep a guy. I don't want to be that girl anymore and to do that I need to move away."

As the words spilled out Shannon heard them through her friend's ears. She sounded like a person stuck in a rut. Someone who was forever looking back.

But she wasn't that person, she reminded herself. She had plans. She was looking ahead. Moving on.

Moving to Chicago.

"I'm sorry." Emma laid her hand on Shannon's shoulder. "I was trying to make you feel better." She held Shannon back, then slowly turned her friend to face her. "I know I wasn't there when Arthur dumped you, but I came to the ranch shortly after that. As we got to know each other better I had always hoped you would tell me more about how you felt. But you didn't and I figured you were a person who didn't dwell in the past and who didn't talk much." She gave Shannon a self-conscious smile. "This is the first time I've heard you say how you feel. I'm sorry for what you've had to deal with. But you're not some poor sod. You're a beautiful woman and any man would be truly blessed to have you in his life."

Shannon held Emma's earnest gaze and felt a warmth ease up into her heart at her friend's little speech. "Thanks for that," she said quietly, allowing a gentle smile to lift her mouth. "You're a good friend."

"So are you. And I don't want you to move away."

Shannon's second thoughts dive-bombed into her mind. She looked past Emma to the mountains surrounding the ranch. Mountains she had ridden up on horseback, climbed and explored with her cousins and her sisters. So many memories were tied not only to this place but to Hartley Creek.

Could she really leave all this?

"I need to do this," Shannon said, though her words didn't hold as much conviction as before.

"But if you and Ben—"

Shannon held up a warning hand.

"I'm just saying," Emma said with a shrug and an innocent look. "Maybe you should ask him to the wedding? Then you don't have to come alone."

"Maybe Shannon should ask who to the wedding?" Carter was asking.

Shannon turned around in time to see her cousin and the very man Emma had been talking about, walking toward them.

"Oh, just girl talk," Emma said with a light wave of her hand.

As Shannon looked over at Ben, however, she couldn't stop a self-conscious blush creeping up her face.

Had he heard?

She looked away, choosing to pretend that he hadn't.

"Thanks for dinner, Emma," she said. "Call me when you want help picking up the candles and decorations."

"Will do," Emma said with a bright voice.

Shannon shot Ben a quick glance. "If you don't mind, I'd like to get back to town before my grandmother comes home."

"Sure thing," Ben said. Instead of letting her get into the truck by herself, he was right at her side opening the door, putting his hand under her arm and helping her into the cab.

At the touch of his warm hand on her bare arm, she flushed again. This was getting ridiculous and she laid the blame for her "flustration" around Ben fully at Emma's feet.

As Ben said his thanks and goodbyes, Shannon caught Emma's not-so-discreet smirk.

She shook her head, then turned ahead just as Ben walked around the front of the truck.

She hoped he hadn't heard what Emma had been talking about. She didn't want him to think she had any designs on him. And there was no way she was asking him to escort her to the wedding.

Chapter Five

As Ben started up the truck, Shannon leaned her head back against the seat, wishing her brain would shut down. Though she had tried to dismiss Emma's comments about Ben, they swirled through Shannon's head.

She knew he was good-looking and she also knew, in spite of her resistance, she had felt those few frissons of attraction.

Emma's comments made her even more self-conscious of those feelings and had succeeded in making her more aware of the man sitting beside her.

She shot him a quick glance, thankful to see he was frowning at the road ahead, concentrating on his driving.

His dark hair and eyes granted Ben a rugged appeal completely at odds with his brother's fair looks.

Arthur of the smiling charm and blond and boyish appeal was a bright contrast to his oh-so-serious brother, who seemed to have a perpetual frown.

She thought of the first time she had met Ben. He had come to Calgary for a medical conference so she and Arthur had driven up from Hartley Creek so that Shannon could meet the brother Arthur spoke so often about.

Ben had appeared distracted and abrupt when they went out for lunch and Shannon had been convinced he didn't approve of her. On the drive home she'd discovered Ben was in the middle of a nasty divorce. His wife, Saskia, had been cheating on him and had served Ben with the papers before he had left for Calgary.

The next time she'd seen Ben was when he came to her apartment to tell her Arthur didn't want to marry her, also not his best moment.

"I really enjoyed dinner," Ben was saying as he made the turn onto the main road leading back to Hartley Creek. "You have a great family."

"They're good people," she said, glancing over at Ben as she replied. But he was looking ahead at the road, one hand on the steering wheel, the other resting on his leg. "I'm thankful for them and all the good times we've had together. I spent a lot of time on that ranch."

"I understand Carter and Garret lived on the ranch with your grandparents?" he asked.

"They grew up there. Auntie Noelle was expecting them when she moved back to the ranch with Nana and Grandpa Beck," Shannon said. "She was a single mom."

"Is she still around?"

"Auntie Noelle died when they were about ten."

"So was she your mom or dad's sister?"

"Auntie Noelle was my mom's sister. My mom moved back to Hartley Creek after my dad divorced her."

Ben turned at that and caught her gaze. "I'm sorry to hear that. Divorce is hard on every member of the family."

Their eyes held, but Shannon was the first to look away, suddenly self-conscious. "It was a while ago," Shannon said with a shrug, touching the gold nugget she wore around her neck. The nugget her nana said she'd given her as a reminder to make better choices than her mother had.

Well, so far Shannon wasn't doing a lot better than her mother. Shannon's father had left her mother after they got married. Arthur had left Shannon before. Just a matter of timing.

"I'm sure it was hard for you, though," Ben continued.

Shannon thought back to that horrible morning when she'd watched her father drive away. Hailey had been downstairs and had come up, crying, telling Shannon that their father was leaving.

He hadn't even said goodbye.

Shannon vividly remembered how she had wanted to cry but hadn't dared because her mother told her she needed Shannon to be strong. To help her with Naomi and Hailey because they were still little.

So Shannon had become the big sister and had helped her mother. When they moved to Hartley Creek, the role expanded as their mother started spending more time away from them.

The bright spots in Shannon's life were her visits to the ranch, where Nana would be in charge and Nana would take control. Neither she nor her sisters ever heard from their father after he left.

Oh, the men in her life, Shannon thought, fingering the gold nugget.

"I can't help but notice your necklace," Ben was saying as trees and hills flowed past the window. "It's quite unusual. Was I imagining things, or do your sister and Emma have the same one?"

Shannon smiled and looked down at the gold nugget. "We got the necklaces from Nana. She gave them to Carter, Hailey and me. Carter gave his to Emma when they got engaged."

"Is there some meaning behind them?"

"I got mine after my nana's heart attack," Shannon said. "She had the necklace made up for me and one each for my other cousins, hoping they would all come back to Hartley Creek to claim them."

"Have they?" Ben asked.

"Carter has. Hailey has. My sister Naomi is making plans to. I don't know about Garret. He was always the one who did whatever he wanted."

"Does the nugget have any significance?"

Shannon smiled as she thought of the legacy the nugget represented. "At one time the five nuggets were charms on a bracelet my nana wore all the time. She got the bracelet from my grandpa, who got the nuggets from his parents, who got them from my great-great-grandfather August Klauer."

"I'm guessing there's a story here," Ben said in an amused tone.

"Yes. There is. All part of our history," Shannon said, smiling at the memory. "My great-great-grandfather August Klauer had traveled across the country from the Maritimes looking for gold. But while he was exploring, he met my great-great-grandmother Kamiskahk. She was from the Kootenay tribe. He fell in love with her and made plans to stay and marry her. Then he discovered she had a pouch of gold nuggets she had received from her father. Her father had told her not to tell any white person about the gold because they would be overcome with greed and would want to know where they came from."

"He was a wise man," Ben said quietly. "I understand there's been a few gold rushes in the area, not particularly helpful to the locals."

"Nor have they been profitable. There's not much gold in the area. At least not right around here." Shannon glanced sidelong at the mountains edging the river. This far past the ranch the valley narrowed; the mountains stood closer to the river as if to guard its secrets. "There's not much gold, but there is coal. Not as shiny or as appealing, but it has been more profitable in the long run."

"So what happened to August?" Ben asked.

"He saw the nuggets and was hit with a bad case of gold fever and even though Kamiskahk pleaded with him to stay and wouldn't tell him where the gold came from, he was determined to find out for himself. So he went out looking. The story goes that after months of fruitless searching, one day he was panning and he felt cold, wet and miserable. He also missed Kamiskahk more than he wanted to look for gold. And he knew he had left a greater treasure behind." Shannon gave Ben an apologetic look. "At least that's the way my nana has always told it. Anyhow, he left his gold pans behind, returned to Kamiskahk and asked if she would take him back. Thankfully for the continuation of the Beck family, she did. The nuggets were passed down through the family and my grandfather was the one who had them made into a bracelet for my nana. And she, in turn, made them into necklaces. She gave one to each of us who have come back, along with a Bible. She said the necklace was to show us where we came from and the Bible was to show us where we should go."

"Does it?"

Shannon shot him a quick frown. "Does what?"

"Does the Bible show you where you should go?"

His bitter tone jarred and surprised her and she thought of the anger in his voice when she'd asked him if he was returning to work in the hospital in Ottawa. She wondered if that had anything to do with his divorce from his wife. She wondered if he felt as abandoned as she had when Arthur had left her.

"I wish sometimes it would be more clear," Shannon admitted with a light sigh. "But I know that when I read my Bible regularly I receive strength and comfort for my daily life. I feel as if God is talking to me through the pages and then I don't feel so alone."

Silence followed this remark and again she looked over at Ben to gauge what he was thinking.

His expression looked melancholy.

"I'm a bit jealous of that," he said, his voice quiet. "God and I haven't exactly been on speaking terms the past few years."

The bleak note in his voice hooked into her heart and gave her courage to ask, "Is that because of your divorce?"

Ben drew in a long breath, his fingers drumming the steering wheel of his truck, his frown deepening. "Saskia was part of it all."

"How long were you married?"

"Two years."

"Any children?"

"Thankfully, no." He let go a short laugh, but it held no humor. "Saskia didn't want kids."

Once again she chanced a glance his way, and once again their eyes met, but he quickly returned them to the winding road they drove down.

Yet in that brief instant Shannon felt it again. The brush of something deeper than attraction. She felt an unclenching deep in her soul. A slow release of a fist that had held a tight rein on her emotions, and before she could stop herself, she suppressed her concerns and asked the next question.

"How did you feel about that?"

His shrug, the universal body language of dismissal, was at odds with the pained look on his face. He waited a moment and Shannon fought the urge to fill the silence.

Then finally… "Looking back it was a good thing we went with what she wanted."

That didn't really answer her question, but she wasn't surprised.

Arthur would have told her even before she asked. Her ex-fiancé had always told her he wasn't the secretive type. That his life was an open book.

Trouble was, his book had few pages.

Ben, on the other hand, held as much back as he could. She felt he released each piece of information with great deliberation and reluctance, which made anything he gave her more valuable.

"What do you mean by that?" she asked, pressing on, curious to hear his answer.

Ben pressed his lips together, then emitted a sigh. "When I met Saskia I was taken in by her looks. She was one of those vibrant, exuberant people who was so different than me. Blonde, blue-eyed, laughing all the time. That old saying about opposites attracting? That was me and Saskia."

As he spoke Shannon felt a thrum of sympathy deep in her soul, keeping time with his words. It was as if he was talking about her and Arthur.

"Is that why you married her?"

"She was the one that proposed, actually," Ben said with an embarrassed laugh. "I should never have gone through with it. Saskia was more in love with the idea that I was a doctor than the reality of what my work required. She thought I would go off to work each morning and come home each night and we'd go out for dinner every weekend." He sent her an oblique look accompanied with a dry laugh. "Which, as you know, didn't happen."

"Dr. Henneson has a cottage on Lake Koocanusa that he's been to about five times in ten years," Shannon said with a sardonic smile. "Occupational hazard."

"Unfortunately Saskia didn't understand that. Created a huge amount of pressure our marriage couldn't withstand. When I found out she was seeing someone else, I knew it was over." He chanced another look her way. "Say what you want about Arthur, but at least he saved you the heartbreak of a broken marriage."

Shannon held his words in her mind, examining them more closely, and she realized he was right. Hard as it had been to be the woman left on her way to the altar, being the woman who was left after marriage would have caused more sorrow.

She had seen that firsthand with her mother. After their father left, Denise Deacon had been rootless, shifting from job to job even after they moved to Hartley Creek. When Hailey was old enough to be on her own, Denise had moved again, this time to Calgary. Neither Shannon nor her sisters heard a lot from her, though she had said she was coming to Carter's wedding.

Shannon was sure much of her mother's restlessness had to do with the humiliation of being left behind. And for the first time in many years, Shannon felt an inkling of sympathy for her mother.

"I think you're right," she said quietly.

She looked his way and as their gazes meshed it was as if the distance between them vanished.

His eyes flicked ahead, then back to her, lingering for a moment, but when his gaze returned to the road, Shannon felt as if something between them stayed connected. With every beat of her heart she became increasingly aware of the man beside her. She tried to banish the feelings. Tried to put them in perspective, but it seemed every time they got together another barrier between them blurred.

Please, Lord, she prayed. *I can't let myself be pulled into these emotions. I have plans and I can't let a man hold my heart in his hands again.*

She drew in a long, slow breath, as if to settle her heart and draw a curtain of protection around it. Her life had finally found equilibrium and she couldn't let Ben Brouwer upset that.

Then the road made a sharp turn and as she forced her attention back to the road, she felt her lips ease into a smile. The tunnel lay ahead and as they drove toward it Shannon leaned forward, waiting. The light was still good. It should be visible.

"What are you looking at?" Ben asked.

"When my grandfather would bring us back to Hartley Creek from the ranch, my sisters and I would have a contest to see who would be the first person to see the Shadow Woman once we got out of the tunnel."

"The what?"

"Just wait. I'll show you." Though she had ridden down this valley countless times, she still felt that little lift of anticipation as they entered the tunnel.

For a second the darkness blinded her and

Ben slowed the truck down. Then a few moments later they emerged into the light again.

The road ahead of them straightened and stretched out, following the hillside down toward the valley that held Hartley Creek.

And there she was.

"There's a pullout just ahead," Shannon said, pointing it out to Ben. "Stop there and I'll show you what I mean."

Ben did as she said and when the truck came to a halt, she got out, wincing again as her foot hit the pavement. She had to do something about that knee. But she caught her balance, then limped around the front of the truck, glancing at the rock face overlooking the town.

A faint breeze coming up from the river below them teased her hair as the cool of the evening drifted into the valley.

"There she is," Shannon said, smiling as the contours and shadows on the cliff face came into view between the hills ahead of them.

"I don't see it," Ben said.

"Those two caves are her eyes and below them a rock jutting out. That's her nose."

Ben frowned, leaning forward as if to see her better, but he shook his head slowly. "I see the caves, but I don't see the face yet."

Shannon moved closer, pointing out the contours. "There's a long shadow that makes her hair and below that, that kind of square shadow, that's her dress. According to my grandmother there's a man also involved in the Shadow Woman legend and that's the dress he bought her."

Ben tilted his head as if to see it from another angle. Shannon glanced his way just as a smile spread over his mouth. "Okay. I see it now. She looks like she's leaning ahead a bit."

"Waiting for the man to return."

"Kind of like your Kamiskahk," Ben said.

"Yeah. Kind of like that. Though my nana had always insisted Kamiskahk wasn't the kind of person to sit around and pine for her lost love. She probably kept herself busy."

"You think so?"

Shannon pushed her hair away from her face and shrugged. "In spite of what Nana said I'm sure part of her waited. Watched the hill he'd walked over when he left, wondering if that flicker in the shadows of the trees was him coming back."

She caught herself, realizing how maudlin she sounded.

"Was that what it was like for you after Arthur left?"

Shannon held his question in her mind, contrasting it with her memories. "I'd be lying if I told you that wasn't true. The first few days, even though I had already called off the wedding, my heart would stop whenever the phone rang, whenever someone came to the door. Each time I thought it was Arthur and he had changed his mind." She blew out a sigh. "I know it sounds silly, but that's how it was for me."

"Again, I'm sorry."

Shannon waved off his apology. "Please don't apologize. It had nothing to do with you and everything to do with false expectations. I suppose, like you and Saskia, I expected something from Arthur he couldn't give me."

Ben looked back at the Shadow Woman and nodded. "Makes for a strained relationship."

"While I'm being completely honest," Shannon continued, leaning back against his truck for support, "I think Arthur's and my relationship had been strained for some time already. I think I hoped being married would change that. Like you said, it was probably better the wedding got canceled."

The mournful wail of the train's horn wafted up to them on the wind coming from the river. Shannon smiled at the sound, as familiar to her as her own face. Sounded like home.

"Is it on time?" Ben asked.

Shannon looked up from her watch. "Sorry?"

"You do that every time a train comes through,"

he said. "Check your watch as if to make sure it's on time."

"One of the few constants in my life," Shannon returned, surprised he had noticed her unconscious habit. Then she pushed herself away from the truck. "But it also means Nana's book club has been done for a while. We should probably get going."

As Shannon turned, she put her foot wrong and pain shot like a hot needle up through her knee. She stumbled and would have fallen but for Ben's hands catching her.

"You're favoring that knee." He frowned as he looked down at her leg. "Are you sure everything's okay?"

"I'm fine," Shannon said. "It's fine." But as she moved to pull away from him, she winced again.

"It's not fine. Come here. Let me have a look at it." With his strong hand still firmly holding her arm, he led her carefully back to her side of the truck. Then, again, he helped her in, but stopped her before she turned.

"Lift up your pant leg and let me see."

She was about to protest again, but she caught his eye and heard the firm note in his voice.

With a sigh she gave in and pulled her pant leg gingerly up and over her knee. "I think it's infected."

"Why didn't you say anything?" he demanded as he carefully unwound the bandage she had put on this morning.

"Why? You're not my doctor."

He shot her a look of irritation. "Maybe not, but I'm still a doctor."

His words hung in the air between them. Shannon's mind jumped back to his touchy response when she mentioned the opening at Hartley Creek.

"That is, I still know how to be a doctor," he said, gently pulling the bandage away from her wound.

Shannon let the comment drop. Though he had said he was taking a break, she got the distinct sense there was more to this than he was saying. The more she got to know Ben, the more complicated he became.

"You're right. It is infected," he said, touching the warm skin around the cut. "Not bad, but you should get it looked at."

He looked up at her and she couldn't look away. The moment lengthened and as she looked into the depths of his brown eyes, Shannon felt a slow awakening of yearnings she thought had died with Arthur's defection.

No. This can't happen. This won't happen. He's Arthur's brother, in case you've forgotten.

Even as the cynical voice called its warning, her heart increased its steady beat. She saw him swallow and wondered where his thoughts were headed.

"It's getting looked at right now by a doctor and an E.R. nurse." Shannon grinned, trying to dispel the emotions of the moment.

Thankfully Ben returned her smile. "I guess you wouldn't get any different treatment at the hospital."

No, but Dr. Henneson wouldn't make her heart go all fluttery when he looked at her.

"I just need to pick up some antibiotic cream at the drugstore," she said. "I didn't have any at home and Emma didn't have any in her medicine cabinet."

"So you snoop through other people's medicine cabinets when you go into their bathroom?" he asked in mock horror as he carefully wrapped the bandage around her knee again.

Shannon laughed, thankful for the return to a lighter tone. "I asked. Besides, Emma is a good friend. She wouldn't be offended."

Ben folded her pant leg over her knee and then pushed himself upright. "It's good to have friends," he said.

"You must miss yours back in Ottawa?"

Ben scratched his chin with his forefinger. "Don't have a lot. It's not that easy to create a circle of friends outside of work. Come to think of it, it's not that easy to create a circle of friends inside work. Besides, any of my friends were also friends with Saskia and unfortunately—" He let the sentence hang between them, then without finishing it, got up and walked back around the truck to his side.

She could guess at what he had been about to say. That in the divorce, many of their friends had sided with his ex-wife.

She felt a touch of sympathy for all he had lost and wondered what had happened in the past year that had made him take time away from an important job and sent him clear across the country to help his mother on her house.

"So where is Saskia now?" she asked.

Ben looked straight ahead, his lips thinning, and Shannon guessed she had ventured into forbidden territory.

"Saskia is dead."

Dread pierced Shannon and she wished she hadn't asked.

"When did she die?" she asked, genuine sorrow for his pain flowing through her.

Ben dragged his hands over his face and expelled a heavy sigh. "A month ago in a car accident."

"Oh, no. I'm so sorry to hear that." She couldn't stop her hand from reaching out and touching his shoulder in sympathy.

To her surprise he reached up and covered her hand with his.

It felt rough, surprising for a doctor, but then he'd been doing manual labor for the past few days. It was also warm and it easily covered hers, giving her a surprising sense of security.

His hand tightened and her heart lifted in response.

"I was sorry, too."

"That must have been difficult."

His grip on her hand tightened. "More than you can know." He gave her an apologetic look. "Sorry, but I don't really want to talk about it."

As he lowered her hand she felt the tiniest moment of loss, then she pulled her hand back, angry with herself for her foolishness.

Yet she sensed there was more to Saskia's accident and death than Ben let on.

It shouldn't matter, she thought, as Ben turned the truck on and pulled back onto the road. Ben's past was none of her business.

But even as she told herself this, a small corner of her soul felt a subtle undertow of dissent. The bleakness in his expression called to her and made her want to comfort him.

She wanted to ask more. Wanted to know more.

She had intruded far enough into his personal life. If she wanted to maintain the distance she felt she needed to around this man, she couldn't ask more. Because she had a niggling feeling if she found out what those bigger reasons were, she would be drawn further into the pain she saw deep in his eyes.

After all the time it had taken to get over Arthur's betrayal, she didn't know if she could allow herself to get involved with Ben. He was far more complicated than Arthur.

But even as she assured herself of this, the optimistic and hopeful part of her wondered what would happen if she allowed Ben into her life.

Chapter Six

Ben lifted the spade and turned over another clump of sod, perspiration running down his forehead into his eyes. He'd been working in the backyard for a couple of hours now, determined to finish by noon. Hopefully the lawn edging would be in at the hardware store by then and he could take care of that today.

Tomorrow he would clip the hedges, pick up some plants from the nursery for the bed he was working on right now, get at that leaky faucet in the bathroom, fix up the window crank on the living-room window and replace all the burnt-out lightbulbs his mother couldn't reach.

The day after that he could get back to work on Mrs. Beck's house. Because on that Wednesday Shannon was going back to work.

Saturday he had come dangerously close to making a fool of himself in front of her. Better to give himself breathing space, and the best way to do that was to wait until she was gone all day before working on the house again.

The sound of a door slamming caught Ben's attention just as he shoved the spade in the dirt.

He wasn't going to look, yet couldn't stop a quick glance over to the other house to see Shannon hobbling down the walk. He wondered how her knee was healing.

And why did that matter to him?

"Do you want to take a break?"

His mother's quiet voice behind him made him jump and almost drop his shovel.

She wore a yellow-and-brown-striped fleece jacket with black stretchy pants today. She looked like a bumblebee ready to do the lotus. Her outfit made him smile, but when he heard Shannon's voice calling for her grandmother, his eyes veered back to her.

He was dismayed to see her looking at him, a frown marring her features.

She was probably wondering why he hadn't come to their house this morning to finish the work he started. He hadn't come because spending time with her on Saturday had made him nervous. Something about her made him talk about things he wanted to push to the bottom of his thoughts and forget.

Being around her made him realize how lonely he really was.

"I'm okay, Mom," he said, gripping his shovel, pushing it into the ground with more force than necessary.

"You said you wanted me to let you know when the lawn edging came in," she continued, ignoring his comment. "Dan just called. I thought we could go together to pick it up."

"Just let me finish up here," he said, grunting as he lifted the next piece of sod. "Then we can go get it."

"How long will you be?"

"About another ten minutes."

"You'll have to take a shower before we go, though."

"Yeah?" He set the spade in the ground again, wondering what his mother was getting at.

"So why don't you have your shower now," she continued. "I hoped we could go right now so I could treat you to lunch at Mug Shots."

Ben glanced at his watch, surprised to see that it was one o'clock already. He gave his mother an appreciative smile. "Thanks, but I can just as easily grab a sandwich here."

Sophie Brouwer made a moue of protest. "I really want to go out for lunch and I don't want to go by myself."

"So go with your new friend, Eloise," he returned, glancing again at the other house.

Shannon was already in the car and as he spoke, Mrs. Beck came out of the house. At the top of the stairs she glanced their way and gave them a polite wave.

Ben couldn't stop the niggle of guilt when he saw her.

"She and Shannon have plans," his mother said. "And I really want to treat you to lunch before we get the lawn edging."

Ben stifled a sigh. His dear mother got stubborn when she latched on to an idea and he suspected her bumblebee outfit was her "going out" clothes.

"Okay. I'll go shower and then we can leave."

Ten minutes later Ben parked his truck across the street from the café, surprised to see so many other vehicles.

"Popular place," he said as he opened the door for his mother and helped her out of the truck.

"It is indeed," Sophie said, beaming up at him. "You never know who'll you'll run into here."

As they crossed the street, Ben couldn't stop his gaze from lifting up to the large church across the street, its brick steeple silhouetted against the blue of the mountains.

Could he see the Shadow Woman from here?

He thought of how Shannon's voice had softened as she spoke of the legend or the ranch, or the town. It wasn't hard to tell that she genuinely loved this place and he wondered if she could leave it all behind as easily as she claimed she could.

As he held the door open for his mother, the mouthwatering scents of coffee and bread assaulted his senses. A row of coffee carafes near the large glass display cases holding premade sandwiches, bagels, croissants and a huge variety of squares and pies.

"So what do you want?" Sophie asked brightly, clutching her purse against her chest.

"I'm not sure." Ben looked at the chalkboards hanging from the ceiling behind the cases, his eyes flicking over the descriptions and prices of all that was available.

"The cranberry, brie and chicken sandwich is wonderful," his mother said. "The turkey croissant is good and so is the Mexican wrap. Mind you, the bacon and cheese bagel is amazing. And oh, you have to try her paninis. So good." His mother kissed her fingers in appreciation. "You have to try the African black bean soup or the chickpea carrot soup. Too bad the wild mushroom soup isn't available today. It's amazing."

Her voice rolled over him as he tried to absorb

all the choices she was recommending. "Sounds like you eat here a lot," he said, his eyes flicking over the sandwiches in the case.

"The food is good and there's always someone I know here. I love the atmosphere." She patted him on the shoulder, then looked up as an older woman wearing a bandanna and a bright orange T-shirt came out of the back of the cafe.

"Hey, Sophie. What can I get you today?" The woman's gaze flicked from his mother to him, a curious light in her eyes.

"Katherine, this is my son, the doctor I was telling you about. He's visiting me for a while. Lives in Ottawa." She reached up and patted him on the shoulder. "He's an emergency-room doctor. Like on that television show *ER*."

Katherine gave him a broad grin. "Welcome to Hartley Creek and welcome to Mug Shots, Dr...." Her voice went up in a question as if asking him to fill in the rest.

"Just Ben," he said with a polite smile. "I'll have the Greek panini, a bowl of the African soup and a cup of coffee."

His mother gave her order, and while Ben paid, his mother tried to protest. He ignored her as he dropped a tip in the cup by the cash register and then took their tray.

As he turned to find a place to sit he saw them. Mrs. Beck and Shannon were at a table in the back corner of the café. Shannon had her back to him, but Nana was looking directly at him. She gave him a smile and wiggled her fingers at them, pointing to the two empty chairs at their table.

Ben glanced at his mother, who was putting cream and sugar in her coffee.

"Picking up the edging, huh?" he asked her, feeling both railroaded and unable to stop a sense of anticipation at the thought of seeing Shannon again.

She gave him a serene smile and without replying, walked past the full tables to the back corner.

"Well, isn't this a lovely surprise?" Mrs. Beck was saying as she pulled out an empty chair beside her. "Shannon, look who's joining us."

Shannon just shook her head, then looked up at Ben. "Such a surprise," she said, her voice laced with irony. "I'm sure you didn't expect to see us here."

Ben had to grin at her sardonic response. "This is quite a coincidence."

"Isn't it?" Mrs. Beck said, the faint sarcasm in both Ben and Shannon's voices seemingly lost on her. "We just got here ourselves. Haven't even prayed for our lunch yet."

"Wonderful. We can do it together," his mother said as she settled herself into the chair.

Ben sat down, as well, shooting a quick glance around the table as the women bowed their heads. He followed suit, looking down at his steaming soup. He hadn't prayed in months and felt foolish doing so in a public place.

Even so, in the small bubble of silence at their table, he felt a gentle nudging in his mind. So he closed his eyes and sent up a quick prayer of thanks for this food. And, while he was at it, a prayer for patience with his mother and her machinations.

When he raised his head it was to see Mrs. Beck giving him an indulgent smile. "So, Ben, what did you think of our pastor's sermon yesterday?"

Her question was followed by a stab of guilt. But he held her guileless expression and said, "I didn't go to church so I didn't hear what the pastor said."

Mrs. Beck frowned. "But your mother—"

"Ben has been struggling with his faith ever since that horrible time in Ottawa," his mother put in, trying to be helpful. Ben wished she wouldn't. Neither Mrs. Beck nor Shannon needed to know anything more than what he chose to tell them himself. Especially not Shannon.

"I'm sorry to hear that," Mrs. Beck was saying. "I know I've had my dry, desert times, but

I also know that I depended on God more then than when things are going well. Do you mind telling me what your mother means about that horrible time?"

Actually, he did. Especially in a public place. Especially in front of Shannon. Then she gave him a sidelong glance and in that look he caught understanding and sympathy.

"You were right about my knee," she put in, forestalling anything he might have to say. "It was infected."

"So my diagnosis proved correct," he said, grasping the conversational straw like a drowning man. "Nice to know all those years of training haven't gone to waste."

"They taught you well in med school," she agreed.

"Ben graduated top of his class, you know," his mother put in. Then Mrs. Beck asked where he went to school and the conversation was diverted.

"We badly need doctors here in Hartley Creek," Mrs. Beck said. "Weren't you telling me that, Shannon?"

"I was," she replied, keeping her attention on her own lunch. "And I'm sure if Ben wanted to, he could get a job here. Hartley Creek is a good place to live."

"So why are you moving?" his mother asked Shannon, putting her on the spot.

Now it was Ben's turn to rescue Shannon. "So when will you be going back to work?"

"Wednesday, according to my actual doctor." Her droll smile made him laugh.

"I'm surprised he let you come to work that soon. You're still not walking properly," her grandmother said. "It would be a shame if you had to limp down the aisle in that beautiful bridesmaid dress Emma picked out for you."

"The wedding isn't until next week Friday. I'll be fine."

"My goodness. That soon?" Mrs. Beck pressed a hand to her chest. "I don't suppose you have an escort yet?"

"I don't suppose you do, either," Shannon returned, giving her grandmother what looked like a warning look.

"I do, in fact." Mrs. Beck inclined her head toward his mother. "Sophie is coming with me."

This was news to Ben.

Mrs. Beck turned back to Shannon. "If you can't find someone, surely—"

"I don't need an escort," she said, as the blush creeping up her face put the sprinkling of freckles on her nose and cheeks in stark relief.

"But, honey. Surely you can't go to the wedding on your own?"

"Surely I can," she protested.

"You wouldn't have been alone if Arthur hadn't broken off your engagement—" Ben's mother stopped herself and Ben could feel Shannon's discomfort growing with each comment.

Afterward he wasn't sure what came over him or why he did it. Maybe because he felt responsible for what his brother did and his own part in the breakup. Or maybe it was because of that moment in the truck on Saturday when something fragile and unnamable had sparked between them, but he turned to Shannon and said, "If you need an escort, I'm available. Seeing as how my mother is going, as well."

The words hung in the shocked silence and Ben could see his mother and Mrs. Beck exchange furtive glances that held a hint of smugness.

But his attention centered on Shannon, who slowly turned to him, her flush deepening.

He had made things worse, he realized as his eyes caught her gaze. He had now put her in an untenable situation. Turning him down would look uncharitable especially in front of his mother.

What had he been thinking? He had put off working on the house because he was growing more uncomfortable around her and now he asked her out on a date?

"I think that's a marvelous idea," Mrs. Beck was saying as Shannon kept her eyes on him.

"Of course, I understand if you would prefer to go alone," Ben hastened to say, giving her an immediate out. "I just thought, after spending time with your family on Saturday, that it would be a fun wedding to attend."

Stop now. Your explanations are making things worse, even though they were true. He had enjoyed being with Shannon's extended family. He had enjoyed watching the give-and-take, the inside jokes, the sentences that would get finished by someone else. He suspected the wedding would be more of the same.

"Of course it will be fun," Mrs. Beck announced. "That's why I asked Sophie to come." Mrs. Beck turned to her granddaughter. "This is the perfect solution. Sophie and Ben can come together because I'll be with Emma before the wedding."

Shannon looked down at the food on her plate, toying absently with her fork, and Ben wished again he hadn't said anything. "I suppose that could work," she said, speaking slowly as if dragging the words out.

Her reluctance made him regret asking her, but there it was. Said and done.

Then she flipped her ponytail over her shoulder and gave him a quick smile. "I accept. Thank you."

He held her gaze and returned her smile. "That's settled then."

"This is excellent," Mrs. Beck said. "I'm so glad we accidentally ran into you this morning."

"Yes. That was a very pleasant and unexpected surprise," Shannon said as she picked up her sandwich. But before she started eating, she gave him a discreet wink.

He was fairly sure she'd meant the wink as a joke. A counterpoint to her grandmother and his mother's transparent meddling.

Yet as their gaze held he felt it again. That indefinable something hinting at possibilities. He didn't want to dwell too deeply on what those possibilities might mean.

For now, though, her accepting his impetuous proposal meant he was obligated to stick around until the wedding at least. Somehow this didn't bother him as much as it would have a couple of weeks ago.

Shannon parked her car, turned off the ignition and laid her head against the headrest of her car, stifling a yawn. The rain sheeting down outside made her reluctant to leave her momentary cocoon.

It was Wednesday, her first day back, and it

had been crazy at the hospital. The rain that had poured down all day seemed to bring out the complaints in the older people and clumsiness in the younger ones.

On top of the usual coughs, colds and intestinal ailments, she'd dealt with two broken arms, a stick in an eye, a sprained wrist, sprained ankle, bruised ribs, one concussion, a dislocated shoulder, a broken collarbone, a cut leg, a cut face and a nail in the foot of a carpenter.

Her own knee still felt stiff, but more than that, she was exhausted. Nana Beck had called to say she wouldn't be home when Shannon arrived. She and Sophie were going to an art show at the old train station and supper was part of the evening's entertainment.

Which left her in the rambling old house to fend for herself. Shannon made a face at the rain streaming down the windows of her car.

One of the reasons she had moved in with her grandmother was to provide her with company in the evenings. She didn't want Nana Beck to be lonely.

Now it looked as if Shannon was the one stuck at home by herself again. Looked like another meal of scrambled eggs. Poor her.

She took a deep breath and sent up a quick prayer. *Forgive me for feeling sorry for my-*

self, she prayed. *I'm just tired and feeling out of sorts.*

The rain gushing down her windshield didn't help.

Well, nothing to be done but face this.

Shannon grabbed her coat and purse, pushed open the door and was immediately assaulted with a blast of cold and wet. She scooted around the front of the car and was headed up the walk when she saw something come sailing off the top of the house onto the lawn at the side.

What in the world was going on?

She shrugged her coat on and as she walked around the side of the house something else came flying down onto the lawn, followed by a loud, steady pounding.

She glanced at the square object lying on the lawn and recognized it to be a roof shingle. She stepped back to get a better view, rain falling on her face making her squint and plastering her hair to her head.

Someone was hunched over on the roof, ignoring the rain pouring down, pounding a hammer.

"Ben? Is that you?" she called out, shielding her eyes with her hand.

The figure lifted his head and then looked down at her. Water ran down his head and his shirt was absolutely soaked, as were his pants.

"I noticed a leak in the roof when I was working in the house," he called out. "So I came up here to check it out. You got a bunch of broken shingles so I'm replacing them. I'll be done in about half an hour."

"But you're getting soaked," she called back, pushing her damp hair away from her face.

"I am soaked," he corrected, his grin a white flash against the dark stubble on his chin, as water dripped down his face. "Can't get any wetter, and I have to finish the job or you'll have more water in your house."

She stared up at him through the curtains of rain, feeling bad that he had to work in this weather.

"Come inside when you're done. I'll make you a cup of coffee," she said, raising her voice above the noise of the rain.

"You got it." He waved his hammer, then returned to his work.

Shannon watched him a few seconds more, then retreated back to the house. Water dripped off her hair and down her neck as she tugged her wet jacket off. Shivering, she hung it on the back of a chair in the front entrance to dry.

As she pushed her wet hair away from her face she caught the aroma of paint. Curious, she stepped into the living room.

The hole in the wall had been repaired and

painted over. It needed one more coat, but already it looked so much better. She checked out the kitchen, as well, pleased to see he'd taken care of that hole, too.

He'd been busy, she thought, and he was still working.

The thought made her feel guilty, especially because she'd been so glad he hadn't shown up here on Monday or Tuesday. Especially after he'd offered to be her escort for Emma and Carter's wedding.

She had tried to be rational about the situation. He was simply being kind. He was helping her out of a cumbersome situation because he was a decent guy.

You didn't have to accept.

On one level she knew that, but as he made the offer and as she looked into his eyes, she had felt an undertow of other emotions that had more to do with the fact that he was a single, attractive man. One she grew more confused around the longer they spent together.

Saying no would have made things easier.

When Emma asked her to be her bridesmaid, the one thing Shannon had dreaded the most was coming to the wedding solo. She knew that as she walked down the aisle as a bridesmaid, people would remember she was supposed to have walked down the same aisle of the same church in a bridal gown. She knew they would think of her as poor Shannon Deacon, still single. Still alone.

And what will people think if you show up with Arthur's brother?

She pressed her cold fingers to her temples. She had to stop analyzing things to death. Ben had asked her. She had accepted. Leave it at that.

She got the kettle on the stove, then took out the cookie tin her grandmother had filled up just the other day. As she put out cups and napkins, her stomach growled and she thought of the banana that had been her meager lunch.

Then she thought of Ben, still working out in the rain, also going home to an empty house. She couldn't only give him a few lousy cookies and some coffee. But what else was available?

She opened the refrigerator to see what she could put together. She doubted cold cereal would do the trick.

Then she saw a large plastic container with a note in her grandmother's handwriting taped to it.

I don't want you to eat cold cereal for supper so I made this soup for you. Enjoy.

"Thank you, Nana," she said with relief. Twenty minutes later the coffee was ready and soup simmered on the stove, sending out enticing aromas that increased the growling in her stomach. She had made a salad and was getting some sandwiches ready to grill when the front door creaked open.

Cold, damp air flowed over the floor as he shut the door behind him.

"Hey there," Ben called out. "Just thought I'd let you know I'm done."

"I'm in the kitchen," she returned. "I got something ready for you to eat."

"Okay. I'll just wash up."

Shannon's hand hovered over the frying pan as a melancholy smile tugged at her mouth. *Gracious, we sound like an old married couple.*

Honey, I'm home. She blushed at the thought.

She knew the second Ben came into the kitchen. She sensed his presence even before he stepped through the doorway.

"Smells good in here," he said. He looked at the place settings on the table, then at her. "What's all this?"

"I found some soup Nana made. I thought you might like something more than just coffee after working out in the cold." She shot him a shy glance, then turned her attention back to the sandwiches sizzling in the pan. "I know that your mom is with my nana at the art show in the old train station so I doubted you would be getting supper tonight unless you made it. If you're anything like me, supper would probably have been cold cereal eaten over the sink."

She was babbling and she knew it, but his presence in the kitchen made her suddenly self-conscious.

"Actually, I prefer scrambled eggs in the living room while watching sports on the television," he said, humor edging his voice.

"Wow. A multitasker."

"Speaking of tasking, anything I can do here?" He took a step closer to the stove, looking over her shoulder.

She caught the scent of rain on his clothes but more than that, was fully aware of his height, the breadth of his shoulders. She was having a more difficult time denying those few moments of connection they had shared. How he had been so concerned about her knee and how he had asked after her. As if he was taking care of her.

An unexpected wave of longing swept through. She had never needed someone to watch over her. She had always been the one who took care of her sisters when their mother decided to take a break from being a mother.

Which happened often.

Even when she and her sisters stayed at the ranch with their nana and grandpa, Shannon had always been the one to make sure the girls went to bed on time, that Naomi ate her snacks and meals on time, that, when they left, they didn't leave anything behind.

And now, in Nana's house, again, she was taking over and taking charge.

Except when Ben was around.

She closed her eyes, her hand clutching the pan as if to anchor herself. Because she was afraid if she didn't she would give in to the weariness that had held her in its relentless grip for the past half year and let herself lean back against him. Let herself depend on his strength instead of her own.

And she knew she could never do that.

Chapter Seven

"Are you okay?"

Ben's hand came up and rested on her shoulder as if steadying her. "You looked like you were going to faint."

Shannon's heart stuttered. Had she actually leaned back into him?

She swallowed at his touch, surprised and dismayed at the confusion created by the feel of his cool hand on her shoulder and by the fact that she had given in to the urge that had washed over her.

"I'm probably just tired," she said with a quick laugh. "Busy day at work."

She jerked her chin at the pan of soup. "If you want to do something, you can put the soup on the table. There's a hot pad ready for it."

"So what kind of things do you deal with at the hospital?" he asked as he reached past her and picked up the soup.

For someone who didn't want to acknowledge his identity as a doctor, his curiosity surprised her.

"I'm sure it's tame compared to the things you've had to do," she said, flipping the last sandwich over to see if it was done. "Today it was clumsy day. Broken bones, sprains, that kind of thing." She put the sandwiches on a plate, brought them to the table.

"We got our share of ordinary, too," Ben said as he stood by the table as if waiting for her. "Where are you sitting?"

"Just here." Shannon pointed to the chair between them as she pulled her apron off.

He pulled the chair out for her, waiting.

The small courtesy surprised her and, at the same time, touched her. She'd never had a man do this before.

She gave him a quick smile of thanks and then sat down. When she was settled, only then did he pull his own chair out and seat himself.

"Thank you," she said quietly, folding her hands on the table in front of her. She paused a moment, not sure what to do. Usually she prayed before her meal, but she thought of Mrs. Brouwer's comment at Mug Shots. How Ben had struggled with his faith.

Should she warn him she was going to pray?

"I know you pray before your meals," he said

finally, as if he'd read her discomfort. "Please. Just go ahead."

She gave him a curious look, surprised at his sensitivity. "Again. Thanks," she said.

Then she bowed her head and closed her eyes, letting her mind shift, putting her attention on the Lord.

"Thank You, Lord, for this food and for the rain," she prayed aloud. "Thank You for the blessing of health and strength and family. Thank You for Your unconditional love that waits for us every day. Help us to honor that love by living a life that shows You in everything we say and do. Help us to share what we have with those who have so much less than we do. Amen."

She waited a moment, as if to let the prayer rest in the quiet between them; then she reached over and lifted the lid off the soup pot.

"This is my nana's famous meatball soup," she said as she held her hand out for his bowl. "She used to make it every Sunday for whoever came over after church."

"My mom made soup every Sunday, too," Ben said, taking the steaming bowl from her. A gentle smile crept over his mouth as if remembering. "Me and Arthur would always come home from church starving and eat three bowls each."

"I understand your mother is a widow," Shannon said as she put the lid back on the pot. "When did your father die?"

Ben stirred his soup with his spoon, looking down at the bowl. "I was thirteen when he died."

"That's young."

"Not much older than you were when your father left." Ben looked over at her. "Though I'm sure your situation was different than mine in the aftermath."

Shannon acknowledged that with a nod of her head. "I don't think my mother ever got over that betrayal."

"How about you?"

Shannon shook some salt in the soup, then carefully set the shaker down. "I was old enough to know his leaving was wrong. Old enough to see how my mother reacted." She glanced over at him and gave him a tight smile. "The women in our family don't deal with disappointment very well."

Silence followed her comment, broken only by the clink of spoons on the bowls as they ate. They both knew exactly what she was talking about.

As the silence stretched, she felt a tension building. She wanted to break the quiet, but wasn't sure what to talk about.

His ex-wife was off-limits for him, Arthur for her.

"By the way, you don't have to take me to the wedding," he finally said. "I know it was an uncomfortable moment, but I wanted to give you an out."

Shannon swallowed a meatball, then gave him another quick look, trying to decipher what he meant. "Are you changing your mind about coming with me?"

"Do you want me to?"

Now they were at an impasse.

Ben laid his spoon down, folded his arms on the table and leaned forward. "Okay. We're acting like this is high school. May as well be up front about this all. I'd like to take you to your cousin's wedding. You're a beautiful girl that I think I could enjoy spending time with. Besides I'm kind of tired of feeling like a loser who doesn't go out at night. At all." He added a smile and as she held his earnest gaze she felt a burden slip off her shoulders. "So maybe I was impetuous in asking you, and maybe it seemed like I did it because I felt sorry for you. Or because I felt responsible for the fact that you were alone—"

She held her hand up to stop him. "We keep going over this. What happened with Arthur was not your fault."

His expression grew serious. "Maybe not. But I still feel like it has been causing some tension."

"It isn't. Arthur made his own decisions and unfortunately forced you to be part of that. Please, don't take on what you don't have to."

"Okay. I won't."

"And for the record, I'm glad you asked to be my escort at the wedding. I know my family really enjoyed having you around on Saturday." This was an understatement. On top of Emma's innuendo when she'd walked Shannon to the truck, her own sister had called her Saturday night telling Shannon she thought Ben was a great guy and it shouldn't matter that he was Arthur's brother.

Shannon had to explain that Ben had come because of Nana and Mrs. Brouwer's clumsy attempt at matchmaking and there was nothing between them, but Hailey pooh-poohed that within seconds.

Even Carter had commented on Sunday that he was surprised Ben wasn't in church with her.

Maybe bringing him to the wedding wasn't the best idea, but she didn't want to dwell on that. Ben had done a lot of work in the house and now on the roof. At the very least she owed him an evening out.

"Good. Then that's settled," Ben said, leaning back in his chair, smiling. "You can also tell your nana this soup is almost as good as my mother's. And that's saying something."

Shannon laughed, thankful for the lightening of the atmosphere.

"So I'm assuming you got the roof fixed," she said as she finished off her soup.

"I'm assuming so, too. When I'm done here, I'll need to check to make sure no more water is coming through the attic."

"How did you notice the leak?"

"When I was working on the kitchen, I noticed a drip coming down the wall so I followed it up to the attic. You'll need to do more work on that roof once the rain stops. There are lots more shingles that need replacing."

Shannon sighed and shook her head once again at her grandmother's hasty purchase. "I have a feeling this house is going to be one work project after another," she said. "I feel bad for Dan and Carter. They're the ones who will have to deal with it when I'm gone. Though if Garret comes back I'm sure he could help."

"So tell me a bit more about your family. I'm intrigued by the cabins at the ranch."

So Shannon did. She told him about the fun she and her cousins had had playing tag, riding horses and throwing sleepovers that involved precious little sleep.

Then she asked him about Arthur, pleased that

it didn't bother her to mention his name. Pleased she could separate Arthur, Ben's brother, from Arthur the ex-boyfriend.

They finished dinner and as they cleaned up, the conversation moved from family to books they liked to read, movies they had watched. As the time slipped by Shannon found herself growing increasingly relaxed around Ben.

The last dish was dried and, as Ben hung up the towel, he glanced at his watch.

As he did Shannon looked at the clock, surprised to see over two hours had passed. She couldn't remember time going by that quickly before.

"I'd like to run upstairs again and have a look at the roof, then I should probably be getting back home. Busy day tomorrow."

"So what's on your agenda tomorrow?" she asked.

"I'd like to put another coat of paint on the walls here and then that's done. If it's not raining my mother has a few jobs for me to do in the yard."

"Any plans after you've got your mother's place shipshape?"

"Not sure. I had thought of heading down to the coast. Do some fishing. Maybe hike the West Coast Trail." Ben scratched his cheek with one index finger, as if drawing his words out. "I have a friend in Portland I'd like to visit. He's promised to take me kayaking."

"What? No golf?" she said with a light laugh. "What kind of doctor are you?"

Ben's smile looked strained and Shannon wished she could take her thoughtless comment back.

"Never did like golf," he said quietly. "So I don't know what kind of doctor that makes me."

He looked up at her and again she caught it. That shadow of pain deep in his eyes.

Leave it be. It's none of your business.

Blame it on a frustration at the return of the unwelcome awkwardness after they had spent such a pleasant few hours together. Blame it on being a big sister. Shannon decided to ignore her rational thoughts.

"What happened, Ben?"

She threw the question out before she could stop herself, plunging directly into the emotional quagmire surrounding any reference to Ben's work as a doctor.

"What do you mean?" he asked, his frown showing her that he had chosen to deliberately misunderstand her.

But she simply leaned back against the counter, her arms folded over her chest. Her classic big-sister pose whenever she'd had to confront Hailey or Naomi about something they'd done.

Something their mother would probably have chosen to ignore.

He dragged his hand over his face, the calluses of his hands rasping over the stubble on his chin, the physical expression of his confusion.

"I know how much time and how much money and how much devotion it takes to become a doctor," Shannon said, keeping her voice pitched low and nonthreatening. "I work with them every day. They may complain about the hours. They may gripe about the patients. But every doctor I work with can't imagine doing anything else." She paused, part of her thinking she should stop there, but the glimpses she had caught of the haunted sorrow in his eyes pushed her onward. "I saw your face when you brought me to the hospital. I saw how you looked around, checking out the equipment, looking over the staff. I got the feeling you would have preferred to be on the other side of the curtain when they stitched up my knee."

She stopped herself there, knowing she had stepped way over the boundaries of their relationship, such as it was.

Ben narrowed his eyes, his hands planted on his hips as he looked past her.

"You don't know what you're saying. You don't know what you're getting into here."

The icy anger in his voice almost made her back down. At the same time, the raw emotion pushed her on.

"Why don't you try me?" She spoke quietly, almost whispering to soften the challenging question.

Ben drummed out a quick rhythm on his hip, then he spun around, facing her.

"Tell me this. Why do you want to know?"

His words battered her and again she was tempted to back down, but they had traveled too far down this path. She had to see this to the end.

Please, Lord. Give me wisdom. Give me the right words. Give me strength.

"I want to know because I think you are foundering right now and that bothers me. I want to know because I think you *are* Dr. Ben Brouwer even though you don't want to be addressed as such. And I'm nosy."

Her lighthearted comment pulled a reluctant smile from him, alleviating the tension of the moment.

Then, to her surprise, he sat down at the table, dropping his head in his hands as he blew out a heavy, heartrending sigh.

She stayed where she was, waiting. Letting the strain of the moment ease.

"All my life I wanted to be a doctor. Ask my mom. She'll tell you how many times I would persuade Arthur to be a victim who I could sew up or resuscitate or operate on." He eased out a smile as if remembering more innocent times in both his and Arthur's lives. "It never left. And you're right. I was completely dedicated to becoming the best doctor I could be. I didn't graduate head of my class, but fairly close. Then I met Saskia and you know how that worked out."

"Actually, you didn't want to talk about that, either."

He released a wry smile. "You're right. I didn't want to talk about that because it's all tied together with me not working as a doctor anymore." He paused, his eyes staring into the middle distance, drawing out the painful memories from another part of his life. "Saskia was unfaithful because she wasn't getting enough time and money from me, though she sure spent enough." This was followed by another humorless laugh. "Anyway, she filed for divorce and I didn't bother contesting. Didn't have the time or energy. It always bothered me that I couldn't give her what she needed. That I wasn't there for her. That I couldn't be the husband she wanted me to be."

Shannon opened her mouth to protest his self-deprecation, but caught herself.

Just listen. Stop being the big sister.

"We had been divorced for about a year when she started calling me again," he continued, leaning back in his chair, his arms folded over his chest. "I wasn't sure what to do about it, but I knew I wasn't getting pulled through that emotional wringer again. The last year of our marriage was one intense meltdown after another." He fell silent and again Shannon had to force herself to keep quiet. To let his words flow out of him at his own pace.

"The first time she called and left a message I called her back, then wished I hadn't. She cried and told me if I had been a better husband she could have been a better wife. She called me every day after that." This was followed by another deep, soul-piercing sigh.

"The day she died, she called me five times before I left for work. I couldn't take it anymore so I shut off my phone. Things were ridiculously busy in the E.R. that day. There had been some serious gang fighting going on and the casualties were flowing into our emergency department. Then Saskia called the hospital. Then she called the phone of one of the nurses working with me that night. Saskia was desperate, she told the nurse. Needed to talk to me right now. I was setting the arm of a man who had been in a fight. He was a drug dealer and a pimp and had been beat up by a man who claimed my patient had killed his brother." Ben closed his eyes, and pressed his hands to his mouth. "Not exactly the cream of society. But I was his doctor. While I was busy with him, Saskia tried to come to the hospital to talk to me face to face. On the way she was hit by a car. She died because I wouldn't leave a simple operation on a man who had done so much bad in the world." He leaned forward, his hands hanging loosely between his legs, then looked up at her, his eyes echoing his sorrow. "That was the day I realized how much being a doctor had cost me."

Shannon listened to his story, her heart twisting at the anguish in his words and expressed on his face. She wanted to say something to take away that pain, but right now the best thing was to silently acknowledge what he had said.

She sat in the chair across from him, took his hands in hers and waited.

"I've paid too high a price for what I do," Ben said finally, his grip tightening on her hands. "All the sacrifices I made, the death I've dealt with, the horrible parts of human life… I thought I was doing good. I thought I was making a difference. But when Saskia died because I couldn't take time away from a man who had probably caused the deaths of some people who came into my E.R.... That's when I took a leave of absence from my work. I couldn't do it anymore. It seemed so pointless. My work as a doctor has cost me too much."

Please, Lord. Help me to say the right thing. Help me to give him what comfort I can.

Shannon waited another moment, then gave his hands another squeeze. "I can't imagine some of the things you've had to deal with," she said, keeping her voice quiet. "I can't imagine how difficult it must have been for you to find out Saskia died while she was on her way to see you." She stopped a moment, not sure if she should say anything more than to affirm what he might be feeling, but it seemed so empty to leave it at that.

She chose her next words with care.

"What I think you need to remember is Saskia also let you down. She made her own decisions in all of this. You weren't married to her, she was no longer your responsibility. You didn't encourage or ask her to come to see you. She made choices in the past that broke the ties of your relationship with her. It was her choices that led to her death, not yours. You were doing the job you had to do, regardless of the recipient."

The silence following her little speech felt weighted with the sorrow Ben had expressed and she wondered if she had gone too far.

Then Ben looked up at her, and in his expression she caught a glimmer of hope. Then a tentative smile curved his lips and he squeezed her hands in return.

"You sound like my counselor," he said quietly.

"Then your counselor is a very smart person," Shannon replied.

This netted her another light laugh. "I'll tell him next time I see him."

Shannon weighed her next question. "Did you start seeing him after Saskia's death?"

To her surprise, Ben shook his head. "No. I was seeing him for a month before that. I was feeling so burnt-out by the job that I knew I needed help. The chaplain at the hospital recommended him so I went."

"Pretty brave of you," she said.

Ben frowned at her. "What do you mean?"

She looked down at their joined hands, feeling the calluses on his palm. She saw a scar across the back of one hand, took in the broken and chipped fingernails. At one time she was sure the nails had been neatly clipped, his hands softer.

Then and now.

The thought created a twist of regret for what he had been and what he had become. Becoming a doctor was a lifelong commitment and he had proved equal to that task. To see him put that aside because of unwarranted guilt bothered her deeply.

"Seeing a counselor voluntarily shows you are willing to acknowledge you can't be everything to all people." She gave him a droll smile. "I've worked with doctors for many years. While they are wonderful people and giving and kind, egos are still involved. The idea that everything should be fixable, treatable. To see a weakness in yourself takes a lot of courage. I applaud you for that."

"Don't applaud too hard," Ben returned, his thumb making small circles over her fingers. "I didn't know where else to go."

Shannon swallowed down a flutter of excitement as each swirl of his thumb smoothed away the common sense and good judgment Shannon prided herself on. She doubted he was aware of what he was doing, but his touch brought out older feelings and emotions she'd thought had died with Arthur's defection.

She knew she should pull her hands away, but she didn't want to break the fragile union expressed in their joined hands.

"I know, as a Christian, you are going to tell

me I should have gone to God," he continued. "But I couldn't."

"I heard an interesting quote," she said, thankful her voice didn't betray her increasing awareness of his hands holding hers. "I don't know where it came from, but it says, sometimes we need Jesus with skin on. Maybe you needed to have someone real minister to you, to show you the way to God."

Just like, right now, she needed the comfort of his skin touching hers.

"That's a good way to put it," Ben said quietly. "Then, I had a hard time seeing God in all the pain and death coming into the E.R. He seemed removed from me. When Saskia died, I couldn't believe He was anywhere close anymore."

He looked up at Shannon and gave her a smile. "So my counselor advised me to take a leave of absence, which I'm doing. And I'm not sure what happens when that's over."

She held his gaze, her heart beginning a slow, heavy pounding. "I think you should go back to being a doctor."

To her surprise, he didn't withdraw from her. Didn't even negate the comment as, she was sure, he might have a couple of days ago.

"Tell me why I should."

His words held a challenge she wasn't sure

she was up to, but she plunged on, going on instinct and hoping to build on what they had established here in this kitchen.

"I'm no counselor and I'm sure he might have told you this, but I read something that really resonated with me. There are two parts to us. How we see ourselves and who we want to be. Often the two aren't the same." She held his gaze, feeling he would listen to what she had to say. "I think you've been trying to tell yourself you're not a doctor. That's how you've been seeing yourself. But so many of the things I see you do, how I see you react, tells me that in spite of not wanting Adam to call you Dr. Ben and despite not wanting to think about being a doctor, really, truly, it's who you are. It's who you want to be. I believe it's who God meant for you to be."

Ben pulled his hands away from her and she felt a trickle of sorrow at the break in the connection. To her surprise, he didn't negate her comment.

In fact he didn't say anything. He sat a moment; then, to her surprise, he reached over and gently brushed her hair away from her face.

His touch sent a tingle racing down her spine and it wasn't as unwelcome as it should have been.

"You're quite a woman, Shannon Deacon.

Full of wisdom and faith and strength. Any man would be lucky—no, blessed—to have you."

His quiet words settled into her heart, easing away old pains and humiliations.

His eyes found hers and she didn't look away. Silence, heavy and expectant, fell on them and Shannon felt as if every beat of her heart thundered in the quiet.

Ben eked out a smile, as his hand cupped her chin. Then he blinked and it was as if a shutter fell down on his features.

"I should go upstairs and see if that roof is still leaking" was all he said.

Shannon tried not to be disappointed as he pushed himself to his feet. What did she expect? That he would raise his hands and exclaim that thanks to her words of wisdom he'd seen the light?

That he would kiss her?

She shook that thought off. She didn't want him to kiss her.

Please be with him, Lord, she prayed as he made his way up the stairs. *Please help him find himself.*

She stayed where she was, choosing not to follow him, though her heart yearned to go after him, to try to find closure to their discussion.

Arthur had always accused her of not giving him space, of trying to organize every aspect of his life. Well, maybe he was right. So instead of following her impulse, she folded her hands in her lap, lowered her head and held him up in prayer.

Right now she could do no more.

Chapter Eight

Looking good, Ben thought, tugging on the shingles he had replaced in the pouring rain yesterday. He sent a quick glance over the rest of the roof and frowned. Though the roof was leak-proof for now, the shingles on this side would have to be replaced in the next year.

He brushed the grit from the shingles off his knees and pushed himself to his feet. As he stood, the mournful wail of the train's horn echoing across the valley caught his attention. He looked over in time to see the train rumbling through the first crossing at the edge of town, the wheels sending out an insistent rhythm that had become familiar to him the past days.

From there his eyes drifted up, as they always did, to the hills beyond the tracks and from there to the large mountain overlooking town where the ski resort was located. Shannon had mentioned that she and her sisters used to snowboard every winter on the mountain with their friends. This, too, was part of the rhythm of the town.

He felt a small twinge of jealousy at the connections Shannon had forged here. The people who were part of her present and past.

Ben's father had worked for a large international corporation that moved him every two or three years to various parts of North America, including one stint overseas in Sweden.

As a result, Ben and Arthur had always been making new friends, establishing new connections. Home, family and community abided wherever his parents and his brother lived.

When his father died, his mother returned to Toronto. After she lost her job there, she'd moved them all back to Ottawa where she had grown up.

When Ben graduated from high school he'd moved back to Toronto for university and med school. Then his mother, alone after Arthur moved out of the house, had asked him to come to Ottawa. Which he had. Then he'd met Saskia, who had moved there from Yellowknife to find a better life.

He let memories of Saskia slip into his mind, thinking, again, of what he and Shannon had spoken of last night. When she'd told him that it wasn't his fault Saskia had died; when she'd said that it was Saskia's choices that had led to her death, not his, he'd felt the first stirrings of relief. Of a weight slipping off his shoulders.

He had tried to fight it, thinking that somehow it wasn't right to release the burden he'd been carrying.

He thought back to the passage his mother read after dinner the other day. From Matthew. *Come to me, all you who are weary and burdened, and I will give you rest.* The part of the passage that resonated the most was, *I am gentle and humble in heart, and you will find rest for your souls.*

The Bible passage stole into his mind and reinforced what Shannon had told him. Rest for a weary soul. Such an elusive thing for him the past few years.

Then he looked around at the town again. From this height he could see the buildings of downtown. If he turned he could see where the river curved and on its banks he caught the glint of a fishing line from a fly fisherman who stood on the bank, his rhythmic casting sending the line into the river.

The shriek of laughter caught his attention as two young boys zipped up the street on their bicycles. One of them saw him and waved.

Peace. That elusive emotion had slowly come

to him here in Hartley Creek, the last place he'd thought he would find it, especially once he found out that Shannon, his brother's ex-fiancée, lived next door.

He smiled, thinking of Shannon. Thinking of the connection they had shared last night and on the trip back from the ranch.

He felt a bond was building between them and he was sure he wasn't the only one aware of it. Last night, when he had held Shannon's hands he'd felt a connection, an awareness. She was easing into his thoughts and into his life.

Then when he had stroked her hair away from her face, he'd felt as if time had wheeled and stopped, waiting for something more to happen between them.

"Did you get all the leaks?"

The sound of Shannon's voice below coming so close on the heels of his wayward thoughts made his heart flop over and his breath quicken.

He walked to the edge of the house and looked down. Shannon looked up at him shading her eyes. She still wore her nurse's scrubs, but her hair hung loose around her shoulders, just the way he liked it best.

"I think I got them all," he said. "But your grandmother will need to do some major roof repair in the next year."

"Why am I not surprised?" she returned with a laugh. "Are you done up there?"

"Yes, I am." He clambered down the ladder, stifling the sense of eagerness her presence brought. At the bottom he took a breath to center his foolish thoughts before turning to her.

She was smiling, her arms folded over her chest. "So, what are your plans for the rest of the day?"

"Not much. Mom wants me to help her rearrange furniture, but she left an hour ago and hasn't come back."

"So, not a real tight schedule?"

"No," he returned with a chuckle.

She nodded, twisting her foot in the grass. "Um, I was wondering if I could ask a favor?" Both her question and her smile were guarded. "I was wondering if I could borrow your truck and, hopefully, you."

Ben smiled at her question. He held his hands out in a gesture of goodwill. "My truck and I are at your disposal."

Her smile solidified. "That would be great. Emma called me at work an hour ago in a huge panic. Carter had to make an emergency trip with a bull to the vet and he's got his truck and stock trailer tied up. She needed some stuff picked up and delivered to the hall for the wedding."

"No problem at all." The thought of spending time with Shannon was more appealing than it ought to be.

"I've got a few things up in my room that need to go, too," she added. "If you don't mind helping me get them down, that would be great."

Ben couldn't help a quick glance at his watch. Four o'clock. "How long will this take?"

"Hopefully not that long," Shannon said as she led the way up to the house. "But if you need to help your mother—"

He held his hand up to stop her. "I think my mother can live with the couch under the window for another day."

Besides, the way his mother and Mrs. Beck had made arrangements for him and Shannon to "meet," he was sure his mother preferred he spend time with Shannon anyhow.

He followed her up the stairs, shooting a quick look into the living room.

"You did a great job on that wall and the one in the kitchen," Shannon said, catching the direction of his glance. "You are a man of many talents."

"True Renaissance man," he replied, giving her a smile.

There it was again. That little spark, that little thrill. Those nebulous beginnings of relationship.

His practical reaction was to brush them

aside, but as her eyes softened and her smile grew, he let his misgivings fade into the background. This was here and this was now. And for now, he was willing to see where things led.

Shannon pushed open the door of her room and hung her purse up on the back of a chair sitting in front of a mirror.

A person's bedroom was like a glimpse into her personality. What he saw of Shannon's room reinforced his own impression of her. Neat. Tidy. Organized.

Yet the framed pictures crowding the top of the dresser, the whimsical figurines parading across a shelf above her bed, the print of a single flower on a mountainside, bending in the wind, also showed a softer side to the woman he was coming to know.

As did the open Bible on the little table beside her bed.

"If you could bring these down for me, we can get them in the truck first," Shannon was saying, grunting as she dragged something across the floor.

He stepped inside the room to help her. She was pulling a cardboard box out of her closet.

"Here, I'll get that," he said, bending over to help her. He grabbed the box, lifted it and as he straightened, he realized he had captured the corner of a plastic garment bag hanging from the back of the closet door. He turned to free himself but pulled the bag loose from the hook and it tumbled down in a heap of white at his feet.

"Sorry about that," he said, looking down, feeling a bit foolish. "I hope I didn't get it dirty."

"Not to worry," Shannon assured him as she pulled the bag free from his arm and gathered up the dress from the floor. "I should get rid of this anyway."

Ben stepped back as she hung it back up again. He felt a touch of dismay when he saw what it was.

Her old wedding dress.

"So that's all I need from here," she said, glancing around the room as if making sure she had everything. She ignored the dress so he thought he should, too. "We can bring this lot down and then head over to the florist's to pick up the pillars."

She marched out of the room ahead of him, a woman with a purpose.

Before he followed her he sent another quick look over his shoulder at the dress now hanging crookedly on the back of Shannon's closet door. The dress she was supposed to wear to marry his brother.

Shannon pushed open the door of the room beside the stage and stepped into the musty interior. She felt along the wall and found the switch. Watery light from a bare bulb barely chased away the shadows in the room.

"We can put most of the stuff in here for now," she told Ben as she pushed aside an empty appliance box that, for some reason, stood in the center of the storage room.

Ben dropped the tall, white column on the floor with a muffled thump. "Thing is heavier than it looks," he muttered, working a kink out of his back.

"I said I would help you," Shannon said, pushing some more boxes out of the way.

"What kind of man am I if I can't carry a white pillar thingy?"

Shannon laughed, then followed Ben as they headed out the door again. "One down, five to go," she encouraged.

"What are they for anyway?" Ben asked as they strode across the hall, their footsteps echoing in the cool empty space.

"The shorter ones are for flower arrangements. The tall ones will have a rod connecting them with a curtain hanging from the rod."

"And that goes...?"

"Behind the head table."

"Carter is okay with all of this?" Ben sounded dumbfounded.

"Carter is so head over heels he's letting

Emma do whatever her little self wants," Shannon said, pushing the door open and stepping out into the bright afternoon light.

"Seems like a lot of work for one night," Ben grumbled as they walked over to his truck.

"Don't tell me you didn't do anything special for your wedding," she teased him.

"Okay, I won't," he replied.

To her surprise he smiled when he said that. Seeing her chance, she asked him, "So what did you and Saskia do for your wedding?"

She almost held her breath when he didn't reply right away. Had she overstepped her boundaries? She thought it would be healthy for him to talk about Saskia. To realize she was a part of his life in other ways.

"Actually, we eloped," he said finally. "Neither her parents or my mother had much money. We figured it was the easiest thing to do."

"So no church wedding? No flowers?" Shannon asked as Ben vaulted up onto the back of the truck and handed her a smaller pillar.

"Saskia had flowers," Ben said. "Can't remember what kind, though." Then he shrugged as he pulled another larger pillar off the truck. "Anyway, it was her and me and a JP and our friends who were married already. Simple."

Shannon felt a twinge of melancholy. Was that why Arthur had balked when she planned her wedding? Had he wanted to do the same thing his brother did?

Her thoughts were interrupted when a car pulled up and two girls spilled out. One of them was Hailey. The other girl was tall and slender, her black hair topped with a fedora, which was a surprising contrast to her long flowing dress and leather sandals. Evangeline Arsenau. The owner of the Book Nook and friend of Emma.

"Hey, girls, high time you showed up," Shannon called out. "We've got to get this truck unloaded and then make one more trip to the ranch to pick up the stuff Emma has for the tables."

"We thought you'd have it all done by now," Hailey called back, pulling a bunch of bags out of the trunk of her car. "Here, Evangeline, can you grab the candles out of the car? Shannon, show me where you want this."

"So what is all this stuff you still have to pick up?" Ben asked as he heaved another pillar out of the truck.

Hailey shot Shannon a concerned glance, which Shannon returned with a shrug. "Most of this was stuff I had bought and got together for…well…for the wedding last year," she told Ben, pleased at the breezy tone in her voice. "My wedding."

Ben held her gaze a moment, then nodded. "Nice that Emma can use them."

"It is, for sure."

Their gazes held a moment longer; then, cheeks flushing, Shannon turned away.

Hailey pulled open the hall door and Shannon stepped inside, thankful for the cool air on her now-heated face.

Hailey had barely let the door fall behind her when she grabbed Shannon's arm and dragged her across the empty hall.

"Okay, did I imagine the goo-goo eyes you and Ben were making at each other just now?" she whispered. Except her whisper was loud enough to echo in the hall.

"Would you be quiet?" Shannon glanced over her shoulder, but thankfully the door behind them was still shut.

"I mean, first he brings you to the ranch, you and him have a little time out just the two of you, and now he's helping you shuttle stuff around for the wedding?"

Shannon wished her heart didn't do that girly tumble thing at Hailey's innuendos. But she would be lying if she said nothing was going on between her and Ben.

"He's a good friend," she replied, pulling open the door of the storage room.

Hailey punched her sister on the shoulder. "You're not a movie star or a pop singer so you're not allowed to vague up your comments. What's the deal? I know there's something going on because Nana said he's taking you to the wedding."

They stepped inside the storage room and as the door fell shut behind them Shannon set the pillar down, then turned to her sister. Now that she and Hailey were in this secluded place, she felt some of her inhibitions lower.

"He's…complicated" was all she said. "Yes, I think I like him, but there's a lot of other things going on and right now I don't need the hassle."

Her sister dropped her head to one side in a "you've got to be kidding" look that was classic Hailey.

"I mean, he's got this guilt over his ex-wife's death and I've got the whole Arthur-dumped-me complex, and the fact that Arthur is his brother…" Shannon lifted her hands and let them drop. "Like I said, complicated."

"He's a single guy. You're a single girl. He obviously likes you. I could see that at the ranch, and you seem to like him. Sounds basic to me," Hailey said.

Shannon frowned at her sister. "When Dan came back to Hartley Creek with little Natasha after his own failed marriage, with your relationship history and all the unresolved guilt over your breakup, would you have let me get away with 'he's a single guy, you're a single girl' schtick you're trying to foist on me?"

Hailey grinned as she flashed her engagement ring. "And look how that turned out. Not so complicated after all."

Shannon bit her lip, realizing she couldn't reason with her sister. Always easier to minimize the difficulties when things turned out well in the end.

Right now Shannon wasn't sure what the end was. She still had her plans and Ben still had his…not plans.

"You're way overthinking this," Hailey said, setting the bags she was carrying beside the pillars. "You do know you're allowed to put yourself first sometimes, my excessively responsible big sister."

Shannon cringed at the words. They seemed so wrong.

"Even when you were engaged to Arthur, you spent more time worrying about me, about Nana, about Naomi, about everyone else but yourself," Hailey said, pressing home her point.

"I'm not that saintly," Shannon protested, folding her arms over her chest.

"Maybe not. But you need to take this one day at a time. Let yourself enjoy being with him. Don't worry about Chicago. Don't worry that he's Arthur's brother. Leave the planning alone for a change. Just let things flow."

Shannon let her sister's words settle into her mind, drew in a slow breath, then jumped as the door of the hall opened. Ben was here.

Her heart fluttered and when she looked at her sister, she realized Hailey had caught her reaction.

Could she really do what her sister had advised? Could she really allow herself to simply take things one step at a time? Not look so far into the future?

Did she dare open her heart again?

Chapter Nine

"What a perfect day for a wedding," Ben's mother was saying as she settled herself in the pew of the church.

Sunshine spilled into the sanctuary through the stained glass windows and as the multicolored beams of light bathed the flowers at the front of the church, Ben had to agree.

"You're looking very handsome," his mother said, flicking a piece of lint off the shoulder of his suit jacket. "I didn't think you even owned a suit."

"I didn't," he admitted. "I bought this from a place in Cranbrook." Shannon had told him the wedding would be more casual than formal and to simply wear what he had.

But after helping Shannon and the other bridesmaids bring all the stuff for the reception to the hall and then, yesterday, helping decorate the church, he was thankful he had taken the time to make the one-hour trip to Cranbrook. This wedding may not be the social event of the year, but it wasn't exactly informal.

Large pots of multicolored flowers decorated the front of the church, flanking two sets of candelabras with white tapers. Yes, Emma had started and grown the flowers herself, but the abundance of them still created an ambience more suited to a jacket and tie than a shirt.

Besides, he knew Shannon would be dressed up and he wanted to honor that by at least looking as formal as she did.

"We were lucky to get this seat," his mother was saying as she glanced around the almost full sanctuary. "I can't believe how many people have come out for this wedding."

Ben couldn't, either. Of course, it had been a few years since he had attended a wedding so he wasn't sure what was considered normal.

Then the ambient music played by the pianist at the front of the church changed rhythm, people grew quiet, and the groomsmen trooped in and stood at the front.

Carter stood with his hands clasped in front of him. Classic groom pose. He was flanked by a man who could only be his twin.

Same dark wavy hair. Same square jaw and piercing blue eyes. Where Carter looked serious, a grin quirked Garret's mouth. Beside Garret was Hailey's future husband, Dan, and beside him a tall man with a shaved head. Matt Thomas, Ben guessed.

As he turned his attention back to Carter he saw him swallow, draw a slow, deep breath as if forcing himself to relax, and for a moment Ben felt sorry for him.

This was why I eloped, he reminded himself.

Then Carter straightened and Ben looked over his shoulder.

Adam and Natasha were the first ones down the aisle. Adam carried a pillow holding the rings and Natasha a tiny bouquet of flowers. They smiled nervously as they rushed along the carpet, obviously in a hurry to get this done.

They were followed by the girl who had helped Shannon and Emma with the decorations, Evangeline Arsenau. Her dark hair was pulled back in a loose ponytail, a dark swath against her apple-green dress. She gave a nervous smile as she took her place at the front.

Then came Hailey, impish grin in place, her reddish hair flashing in the light. She grinned at Carter as she took her place beside Evangeline.

When Ben turned back to see Shannon walking down the aisle, he could do nothing but stare.

Her hair was drawn away from her face on

one side, spilling in a riot of auburn curls over her shoulder. The green of the dress emphasized her hazel eyes and the way its full skirt flowed as she walked gave her an ethereal look that made him swallow.

"She's so beautiful," he heard his mother whisper beside him.

Ben knew she wasn't talking about the bride stepping through the doorway into the aisle.

The rest of the congregation watched as Emma floated down the aisle on the arm of a shorter, squat man who Ben guessed was Wade Klauer, the foreman of Carter's ranch, but Ben's attention rested solely on Shannon as she took her place at the front.

The music stopped when Emma and Wade made it to the front of the church; the minister stepped forward and the service began.

Emma and Carter had eyes only for each other and in spite of the distraction of Shannon standing beside Emma, Ben couldn't help but be drawn in to the obvious love these two had for each other. He knew their story. Shannon had filled him in on the way to the ranch.

Emma was a single mother of Adam, the young ring bearer, and Carter had lost his son when he was Adam's age. In a rage of grief Carter had left the ranch for two years only to return when Nana Beck had her heart attack.

And he and Emma had fallen in love as they worked together on the ranch.

Their feelings for each other were on full-and-unabashed display as Carter's deep voice rang out declaring his promises to care for this woman, help raise Adam, and nurture her, Adam and their future family in their faith.

Emma's voice was quieter and wavered a time or two, but her declaration was equally heartfelt.

Ben found himself strangely moved by the vows and as they were spoken, his gaze slipped over to Shannon to catch her reaction.

What was going through her mind right now? Was she sad? Was she thinking about her own aborted wedding? Less than a year ago she was supposed to have been standing here making the same promises.

Wearing the dress that still hung in her room.

He saw Shannon swallow and surreptitiously reach up to catch an errant tear, and when she lowered her hand her gaze shifted to him.

Everything around them slipped away, became meaningless, and Ben felt as if the air in the church had suddenly diminished.

She was so beautiful, he thought. But she was more than that. She had a depth of character and the conviction of her faith.

Then Shannon lowered her head to break the

connection and Ben reluctantly drew his attention back to the minister.

"Carter and Emma have made promises to each other today," the minister was saying. "An old saying goes, 'love is the blessing on promises kept.' Too many times we think we need love to keep promises, when really it is the other way around. God's love for us as individuals is shown in the promises He keeps to us. The promise that all the burdens we carry, all the sins we have committed are all taken away in the promise of His Son's death. Love is personified by keeping promises."

The pastor's words sifted into Ben's consciousness, seeped into his soul.

He had kept his promises to Saskia. She hadn't kept hers to him. As Shannon had said, he hadn't failed Saskia. She had failed him.

Saskia made her own choices.

Shannon's words echoed in his mind and as he leaned back in the pew, he felt as if he had released a lingering grip on the burdens he had carried.

"Carter and Emma have both had hard times in their past and God does not promise them, or us, that there won't be hard times ahead," the pastor was saying. "But He does promise to hold us through those times. To show Himself to us if we open our hearts to Him. If we open ourselves to the outpouring of His love. Only then can we experience His extravagant love."

As the pastor spoke it was as if his words seeped into the parched and weary parts of Ben's soul, nourishing and refreshing. God had become a shadowy part of Ben's past. Someone he had heard stories about and had, at one time, prayed his innocent prayers to. Someone who had slowly become overshadowed and lost as Ben became immersed in the hard and dirty business of emergency-department work.

In the past few days, however, it was as if Ben had become immersed in nature. Each time he looked up to the mountains, each time he heard the wind in the trees behind his mother's property, it was as if God was silently, quietly moving back into his consciousness, like an antidote to the sorrow that had permeated his life the past few years.

And now, as the preacher spoke these words, Ben was reminded that he may ignore God, but that didn't mean God didn't exist.

Old memories fought back. The pain and misery of the people he worked with in the E.R.

And yet…

He closed his eyes a moment, as a prayer floated up through the layers of his consciousness he had built up to keep God out. To keep love out.

Forgive me, Lord, he prayed. *Forgive me for keeping You out of my life. Forgive me for being so arrogant as to think that my doubts of Your reality could erase it. Forgive me for not seeing Your love.*

He paused a moment; then as he looked up, he caught Shannon's gaze. The faint frown of questioning. He gave her a quick smile and a nod, to let her know all was well.

As he held her gaze, he realized that for the first time in a long time, all was indeed well. Both with his soul and with his life.

"So tell me about this Ben guy," Garret was saying as he swept Shannon once more around the dance floor of the hall. "And tell me what's so important about him that you aren't even listening to your nearest and dearest cousin."

Shame warmed her cheeks as she dragged her attention away from Ben, who sat at a table with her grandmother, Dan, Adam and Natasha. Adam had ditched his tuxedo jacket and bow tie and had parked himself right beside Ben. From what Shannon could see, the little boy peppered Ben with questions.

Ben was smiling, so as far as Shannon could tell, he didn't mind.

"There's not a lot to tell," Shannon said, dragging her attention back to her handsome cousin.

"He's helping his mother fix up her house, which happens to be next door to Nana's new house."

"Convenient," Garret said with a smirk.

"Very," Shannon agreed, unable to keep the ironic tone out of her voice.

They made another turn and once again Shannon glanced over at Ben to catch him watching her. And smiling.

"I haven't seen you smile like that in a long time," Garret said, giving her hand a teasing squeeze. "Looks like something special might be brewing between you and the good doctor."

Shannon didn't have to say anything. She was sure her blush told her cousin all he needed to know.

"So, it's not too weird that he's Arthur's brother?" Garret asked, voicing Shannon's own main concern.

Shannon held the thought a moment, weighing it, measuring it against her current emotions. "It was at first. But he's getting to be less Arthur's brother. He's just, I don't know, Ben."

Garret laughed. "I don't think there's any 'just' with this guy."

Again, Shannon didn't say anything. For one thing she didn't need to give Garret any more ammunition. And for another, everything between her and Ben seemed so tentative, so fragile; she wasn't sure where, if anywhere, things were going.

As she had told Hailey, she still had her plans and she wasn't sure she wanted to rearrange her life, again, around a man.

"How are things with you on the love-life front?" Shannon asked, diverting her cousin's attention away from herself and back to him.

Garrett's only response was a shrug. His default reply whenever he didn't want to answer a question.

"I guess nothing is happening with your most recent girlfriend?"

"We broke up. I wasn't making enough money for her," he said with a laconic smile.

The music ended, and Garrett tucked her arm in his and led her back to her table, then looked down at Ben, frowning. "So here she is, safe and sound," he said, a warning note in his voice. "Make sure you keep her that way."

Shannon wanted to punch him for saying that. Yet at the same time his comment to Ben warmed her heart. It was good to have family looking after you.

"I'll do my best" was all Ben said in reply.

Garrett pulled Shannon close, gave her a light kiss on her cheek then reluctantly let go of her. He touched her nose with his index finger like he used to when they were younger, then said to her, "You know I'm always here for you."

Shannon heard the concern in his voice and gave him a quick smile. "I can take care of myself."

"Just make sure you do," Garrett said. Then he walked away to join a group of laughing friends.

As she settled herself down at the table, Adam accosted her.

"Is it okay I took my tie off?" Adam asked, fidgeting with the collar of his shirt. "Dr. Ben helped me."

Shannon gave "Dr. Ben" a quick smile. Then turned back to Adam. "You and Natasha did a really good job today," she said.

"That's what Dr. Ben said, too." Adam beamed at his new friend.

"Sorry for having to leave you with all the relatives," Shannon said to Ben. "Emma and Carter wanted all of us at the head table for dinner. Now all my obligations are done, I can rescue you."

"I didn't mind," he said. "Adam was telling me all about the ranch and Natasha was saying how she and Hailey are going biking tomorrow after church. She said I could come, too."

"I got a new bike," Natasha put in, resting her chin on her stacked hands. "I wanted to ride it today, but my dad said if I fell and scraped myself, I wouldn't look nice for the wedding." She swung her legs back and forth, giving Shannon an appraising look. "You look really pretty, Auntie Shannon. Like a princess."

Her offhand compliment warmed Shannon's heart.

"I would have to agree," Ben said.

His compliment did more than warm her heart.

Then he turned to Adam and Natasha. "I hope you kids don't mind, but I would like to have a dance with your Auntie Shannon."

Shannon's heart did a funny little jump as he turned to her.

"If that's okay with you," he said to Shannon.

"Sure," Natasha replied, thinking he spoke to her.

"When you come back, you can tell me about how you had to cut that man's leg off," Adam called out.

"What in the world?" Shannon spluttered as Ben drew her to her feet.

"Seems he's very interested in some of the more gruesome aspects of my work." Ben shook his head as he led her to the dance floor.

She felt confusion as Ben turned her around, then took her hand in his and placed his other hand on her waist, leaving her to rest her free hand on his shoulder.

The music was a lively country song. Thankfully it was a two-step, something she and Hailey and Naomi practiced with Garret and Carter as kids whenever they went to the ranch.

As Ben found the rhythm and Shannon followed, she tried to pretend it was just another Saturday night at the ranch. And that she wasn't dancing with this darkly handsome man, but with Carter or Garret.

Only Carter or Garret never made her senses reel the way Ben did. The touch of Ben's hand on her waist was nothing like the impersonal one of her cousins.

The way he looked down at her was certainly nothing like what she'd experienced with her cousins.

"Are you having a good time?" she asked above the music, disappointed at the breathless tone of her voice, but determined to keep the conversation light and casual.

"I'm really enjoying myself. It's fun to watch the interactions of the people here," he said, glancing around the room and the now-crowded dance floor. His eyes returned to hers. "It's obvious the people here know each other very well. There's something really encouraging about that."

"It has its good and bad," Shannon said, thinking of the comment she overheard in the washroom of the hall right after dinner. An old friend of Hailey's was asking another woman if she knew anything about this Ben guy who was Shannon Deacon's escort to the wedding. Wasn't he Arthur's brother? Didn't she think it strange that Shannon would take him along to a wedding barely a year after Arthur dumped her?

The conversation faded away as the women left, but Shannon stayed a moment longer, her ears burning and her heart pounding, reminding her why she had to leave town.

Now, as she danced with Ben, as she felt his hand in hers, her emotions grew even more conflicted. With Ben she felt different. Safe.

A tiny, somewhat shallow, part of her felt proud that this man was with her. That after being rejected and pushed away, this appealing man had asked to be her escort to this wedding.

She looked up at him and as their eyes met a smile slipped over his features. Then the lights went low and the music changed tempo and flowed into a waltz.

Her heart flopped over as their eyes held, then thundered as he pulled her close and their steps slowed. She swallowed as he tucked her hand against his chest. Uncertain of what to do she held herself away from him for a few beats.

But her lonely heart and the attraction she knew was building between them wore down her resistance, and she drifted against him with one easy motion, closing the small distance between them.

Their steps were in sync, so easy, so smooth. As if they had been dancing partners all of their lives.

This feels right, Shannon thought. *His arms feel like home.*

She could feel his steady heartbeat through the fabric of his suit and she wondered if he could feel hers.

Then, too soon, the music stopped and again, changed tempo. Reluctantly Shannon pulled away from him and once again looked up to catch him gazing down at her.

"Let's go outside," he said quietly, still holding her close.

She said nothing, only nodded and allowed him to lead her out a side door, away from the buzzing noise and warmth of the crowded hall.

As the heavy metal door of the hall fell shut behind them, closing off the noise with a click, it was as if they had entered another world. The cool evening air wafted over her and the dusk of the setting sun hinted at secret possibilities.

Ben caught her hand and glanced down at her delicate sandals. "Can you walk in those?"

"Depends on where you want to go?"

He angled his chin toward a path. "I'd like to go down to the river."

"I can get there," she said, surprised at how breathless she suddenly felt.

Ben's hand tightened on hers as he led her down the narrow path. Branches tugged at the gauzy material of her skirt and brushed her bare arms, and dragonflies buzzed around them, chasing elusive bugs. The gurgling of the river grew louder as they slowly made their way down the rocky path.

Shannon slipped once and would have fallen, but Ben caught her by the arm and righted her.

"You okay?" he asked.

"I'm fine. Just keep going."

They broke through the underbrush, and then they stood on the banks of the river. The water sighed and burbled over the rocks as Ben led her across the sand to a dry log that looked as if it had had washed up on the shore years ago.

Shannon settled herself on the log, then reached down and tugged her sandals off.

"That feels better," she said with a sigh as she wiggled her feet in the cool sand.

"Can't see how you can walk on those things, let alone dance in them," Ben commented as he unbuttoned his jacket and set it on the log beside him.

"Determination," she said with a light laugh. "And pride. Can't fall down in front of all the people."

Ben chuckled as he loosened his tie.

"By the way, sharp-looking suit," she said, taking a chance and touching him on the shoulder. "I don't imagine you packed that in your luggage."

"It's new," he said, setting his tie aside and rolling up his shirt sleeves. "You said it was casual, but I knew you'd be dressed up and didn't want to let you outshine me." He added a broad smile, to let her know he was kidding.

Then as he looked at her his smile slowly faded and his expression grew intent.

"You look beautiful." His voice was husky, giving a certain gravitas to his compliment.

"Thank you." It was all she could say.

Then he reached over and touched her hair. "I'm glad you wore it down," he said, letting his fingers drift down.

Shannon swallowed down a sudden rush of emotions. What was going on here? Why was she letting him do this?

As she looked into his eyes she knew that whatever had been building between them would be expressed. Soon.

She pushed away second thoughts. Denied the

questions that had clamored in the back of her mind all through their dance together.

Right now it was just her and Ben, sitting on the side of the river. The same river she and her cousins had played in farther upstream. The same river she had stood beside only a year ago, shedding tears that had become a part of the river's ceaseless flowing.

The river and time flow on, she thought. What she thought she couldn't endure had simply become part of her past.

And now?

"Where are you?" he asked, his fingers now lingering on her cheek.

She let a melancholy smile slip over her lips and she took a chance and reached up, anchoring his hand in hers.

"I'm just thinking about time. How it really does heal wounds." She held his gaze, hoping he realized what she was trying to say. "How I'm glad you came to the wedding with me."

"I'm glad, too," he said. "I really appreciated what the pastor had to say. How God's love is abundant and persistent. It's been hard for me to see that, but thanks to you it's much clearer now."

His words settled in her heart, making a home there, relieving her last misgiving about him.

Her hand tightened on his and then on the

banks of the Morrissey River, Ben Brouwer kissed her.

The gentle touching of his lips to hers was so light she might have imagined it.

As he drew back and she saw how his eyes had darkened, and she knew it was just a prelude. She felt her heart quicken.

This time when he lowered his head, she slipped her hands around his neck, anchoring herself to him. His mouth moved over hers, a union, a blessing underlined when his arms held her close to him and their hearts seemed to beat as one.

Time wheeled and stilled.

Then, slowly, the murmuring of the river and the wind sifting through the trees above filled her senses, bringing back reality.

Shannon was the first to pull away, utterly bemused by what had just happened. She had spent less time with Ben than she ever had with Arthur and yet, this first kiss from Ben felt more right than any she had from her ex-fiancé.

Ben laid his forehead against hers as if unwilling to break their connection.

Neither of them spoke for a while, letting the experience settle as the river flowed on beside them, splashing against the rocks at the edge, cooling the air around them.

Shannon didn't want to overanalyze the moment. It was too wonderful. Too pure, almost.

Then Ben drew back, his fingers trailing down her face.

"I hope you know how special you are," he said quietly, a tinge of awe in his voice.

She wanted to make a joke to ease the tension of the moment, but for some reason, couldn't find her breath.

"For the first time in a long time I feel at peace," Ben continued. "A peace I have only felt around you."

Shannon gave him a careful smile and cupped his face in her hands. "You make me feel special," she said quietly, amazed at how natural it felt to touch him. To lay claim to him.

He brushed another kiss over her forehead. Just a light touch, but the casualness of it underlined the change in their relationship.

Then he caught her hands in his and held them on his lap. He stroked her fingers with his thumb, his eyes following their movements.

"So, I guess things are different between us now," he said quietly.

"I guess" was all Shannon could say.

"I didn't plan on this when I offered to escort you to this wedding—I want you to understand that."

"Well, it's a wedding. Sometimes funny things happen—"

"No. It's not that," he said, his voice holding a serious note. His gaze focused on her. "I know I'm not being arrogant when I say that I'm sure this isn't a spur-of-the-moment thing for you, either. You're not the kind of girl that gets caught up in the emotion of the moment."

"Occupational hazard," she said with a light laugh. Then she grew serious. "No. This isn't some spur-of-the-moment thing and to tell you the truth, it scares me. I'm not sure what I'm allowed to think or what I'm supposed to feel."

His hands tightened on hers. "Why don't you just go with what you want to feel?"

She caught his gaze and then smiled. "I want to tell you that I feel wonderful around you. I want to feel that what is happening between us is right. Because deep inside of me, that's what I really feel."

Ben's smile warmed her soul.

"So do I."

They sat quietly for a long moment, as if letting everything that had happened settle into their being. Become normal.

Because Shannon knew the moment they returned to the hall, her cousins, her grandmother and anyone who knew her well enough would be able to read her like a dime-store novel.

They would all know that Ben Brouwer had kissed her. And that she had enjoyed every second.

"I suppose we should be getting back," Ben said finally, tucking his tie in the suit pocket of his coat.

Shannon sighed her reluctance. "I suppose. I'm sure people are wondering what is going on."

"I think they know exactly what is going on," he said. Then he touched her on the shoulder. "I'd really like to take you to church tomorrow," he said. "Would that be okay?"

Her errant heart gave another quick beat. "That would be wonderful."

"I'm hoping," he replied.

Then he bent over and picked up her sandals. "Give me your foot," he said as he knelt down in front of her.

As she lifted her foot she looked down at his bent head, gave in to an impulse and ran her fingers over his dark hair.

"You're distracting me," he said in a gruff voice as he struggled with the tiny buckles of the sandal. She was about to take it away from him when he managed to get it fastened.

"Pretty good for a guy," she said with a laugh.

"I'm a doctor. I'm supposed to have steady hands."

His acknowledgement of that fact gave her

pause, and the smile he gave her as he slipped her shoes on her feet gave her hope.

"There you go, Cinderella," he said as he tied up the last tiny buckle.

Shannon held her foot out as if to inspect his work, then nodded her approval. "Well done, Prince Charming."

He chuckled as he brushed the sand off his knees, then caught her hand and tugged her to her feet. "So, should we go face the music? Literally and figuratively?" He hooked the fingers of his other hand into the collar of his suit coat and flipped it over his shoulder.

"As long as I only have to dance with you," she said, clutching his hand as he helped her along the sand.

"That's a promise I'll gladly keep," he replied.

Yet, as they headed toward the hall, in spite of the magic of the moments they had just shared, misgivings tugged at her with each wobbly step she took in her flimsy sandals.

Was she being smart about this? Or was she hoping Ben would heal the wounds his brother inflicted?

Chapter Ten

Shannon let the words of the final song of the church service anchor themselves in her soul.

His purposes will ripen fast, unfolding every hour. The bud may have a bitter taste, but sweet will be the flower.

Church had always been one of the few places where her heart was still. Somehow, with Ben standing beside her, her heart was anything but still.

It sung, it rejoiced, it fluttered with every touch of Ben's hand on hers, with every sidelong glance.

Many times during the service she'd had to ask for forgiveness for her distraction. Now, again, she glanced over at Ben standing beside her, his hand supporting the hymn book. He had a deep, baritone singing voice. Strong. Sure.

Considering what he had said about God before, he seemed to be listening intently to what the pastor had to say.

As did she. The words they'd just sung echoed where she was in her life. What Arthur had done to her had created a bitterness in her soul, but being with Ben made her feel as if the rocky path she had been walking had brought her to this moment. This precarious happiness she didn't dare examine or hold too closely for fear it would slip away from her like water through her fingers.

As the last notes of the song faded away, the pastor lifted his hands and pronounced the benediction on them.

Church was over.

The pianist and the band played the postlude as the buzz of conversation increased, overcoming the music.

Shannon turned to Ben, who was watching her, a bemused expression on his face.

"What?" she asked, nudging him with her arm.

"I'm trying to figure out how you managed to keep your hair looking exactly the same way it did yesterday." He touched the flower she had pulled from her bouquet this morning and, on impulse, tucked in her hair.

"I slept sitting up," she teased.

He laughed and the sound created an answering warmth in her heart.

"By the way, you don't have to come to the barbecue after church," Shannon said, as they waited for his mother to finish chatting with the woman in front of them.

"I don't mind," he replied, rolling up the bulletin they had received when the entered the church. "My mother really wants to go and I'm sure your nana does, as well."

"Okay. As long as you're sure."

"Hey, it's a way of being with you." Ben's comment and accompanying wink were playful and lighthearted and added another dimension to their relationship.

Being with you. Shannon tested those words, turning them over to see what was on the other side.

Stop it, she told herself. *Leave things be. Stop looking so far ahead.*

Arthur had always accused her of living with her day timer in one hand, her pen in the other. Maybe he'd been right. Maybe she did like things too neat and laid out. Maybe she should just let what happened between her and Ben happen.

Mrs. Brouwer was finally finished talking, but as she and Ben made their way into the aisle, Alana Lavale, an old friend, caught her by the arm.

"How was the wedding?" she asked, her platinum-blond hair swinging over her face. "I heard it was very romantic."

"It was beautiful," Shannon agreed.

"Of course Garret came?" Her question held a faint note of urgency that made Shannon think this was the real reason Alana had waylaid her. "Is he still around?"

"He left early this morning. He had some big meeting with an investment adviser in Calgary."

Alana's hazel eyes narrowed as she nodded. "That's good. Larissa left for the weekend because she knew he would be around, but she's home this afternoon."

Shannon only nodded, unwilling to be drawn into this particular drama.

Larissa and Garret had dated in high school and all she knew was that Larissa's father, who did not approve of Garret for his darling daughter, had gotten wind of the relationship and found a way to end it.

But the way Alana was talking, it was as if her friend was the injured party.

"I heard you were buying Chocoholics on Main Street," Shannon said, shifting the topic as she and Ben made their way down the aisle, Alana walking beside Shannon.

"I'm in the process," Alana said, her face growing suddenly animated.

Shannon asked a few more questions and Alana launched into a detailed explanation of the business, what was involved in buying a franchise and how she planned to change it.

As they walked Shannon caught Ben glance over at her, an ironic smile on his face. She was going to ask him what that was all about later, but for now she kept her attention on Alana.

By the time they got to the foyer, Megan Tolsma, a friend of Hailey and Shannon's, had joined them and the conversation moved back to the wedding again.

As they talked, though, Shannon could see both girls cast curious glances from her to Ben, as if trying to puzzle out the relationship.

Then, when Alana left and Ben got waylaid by Dan and Hailey, Megan leaned closer to Shannon.

Don't get defensive, she reminded herself, relaxing the tension she could feel building in her neck. *Don't let her fuss at you because he's Arthur's brother. There's nothing weird about it.*

"So, this Ben guy, quite a looker," she said with an approving note in her voice.

Shannon relaxed, but only a bit. This was Hartley Creek, after all, where short memories were jogged by the people with long memories.

"Is he a friend, or is it something else...?" Megan let the sentence fade away, as if waiting for Shannon to finish her thought.

"It is what it is" was all Shannon would say, glancing over at Ben, hoping he hadn't heard, hoping Megan wouldn't make the obvious comment about Ben being Arthur's brother.

"You sound like Hailey," Megan said with a sigh. "Or any of my grade-one kids."

Shannon just laughed, feeling relieved at the turn of the conversation.

"Well, I hope he takes care of you," Megan said, shooting him a frown, as if warning him in case he looked their way.

"I can take care of myself," Shannon replied.

Megan angled her head to one side, giving her a bemused look. "We all know that. Sometimes it's nice to have someone take care of you for a change." Megan patted Shannon on the shoulder. "I should go. I promised I'd flip burgers for the barbecue. You coming?"

"I think so," Shannon said. "If Ben wants to."

"Looks like Hailey is convincing him to stay," Megan replied, slipping her purse over her arm. "Catch you later."

Shannon looked over to her sister, who was clinging to Ben's arm, her face holding that pleading look Hailey had down to an art.

"You'll really enjoy it and the food will be

great. I promise," Hailey was saying. "I think Kerry donated a bunch of pies, which are amazing in their awesomeness."

"Leave him alone," Shannon told her sister as she joined them. "Your nagging is unnecessary. We're going."

Hailey immediately let go of Ben's arm. "Well, that's just peachy keen," she said, giving her sister a broad smirk.

"You know, for a teacher, your vocabulary is rather limited," Shannon said, forestalling any other comment her unpredictable sister might make.

"My vocabulary is precisely pitched to my audience. The sensibilities of grade-two children need not be inundated with multisyllabic words," Hailey returned, giving her sister a playful nudge with her elbow to show that Hailey wasn't done with her and Ben. Yet.

"I smell burgers," Natasha said, pulling on Dan's arm. "And I'm hungry."

"I echo the sentiment," Hailey said. She tucked her arm into Dan's and together they left.

Shannon waited a moment, as if to give her some buffer space from her sister, then turned to Ben.

"Are you sure about this? You still have a chance to back out."

Ben grinned down at her. "I'm sure. I think it will be a lot of fun."

"Okay. But this is a small town where everybody knows everybody's business." The comment she had overheard in the bathroom at the wedding hung at the back of her mind. "Just be prepared for, well…" She paused, trying to find the right way to tell him what to expect.

"Comments? Questions? People wondering what a gorgeous girl like you is doing with a homely guy like me?" He angled her a crooked smile.

Shannon felt her misgivings fade away in the face of his humor. "Something like that. Except for the homely-guy part."

He shrugged her concerns aside. "I can hold my own."

With that confident comment ringing in her ears, the two of them stepped out of the church. Before they crossed the street to the park where the picnic was being held, Ben caught her hand in his. He gave it a squeeze and together they walked across the street.

"I know your mother absolutely loves having you around," Angela Beattie, an elderly lady, was saying to Ben as he forked the last bite of pie into his mouth.

The barbecue was still going strong, but he

already had eaten a burger and turned down a hot dog and was finishing off his second piece of pie. The pecan had been recommended by Shannon; the lemon meringue he held now had been foisted on him by Angela, a friend of his mother's from book club.

"Your mother was telling us at book club that you're a doctor?" Angela fairly beamed up at him, her wrinkles almost obscuring her bright blue eyes. "I know we sure could use a doctor around here. We're so short at the hospital, though I'm sure young Shannon could tell you that very same thing." Angela patted his hand. "Why, I think you should apply. I'm sure you'd get a job lickety-split."

Ben wiped his mouth with his napkin, holding his plate with the other and simply nodded in response. "I probably could" was all he could say.

Angela reached out to take his plate. "Here, I'll take care of that. Could I interest you in some banana cream? Kerry makes the best banana cream pie. It melts in your mouth."

Ben held up his hand. "No. Thanks. I'm full."

"Some blackberry cobbler?"

He shook his head, glancing around the people milling about the park, looking for Shannon. Couples stood in the bright sunshine, older people sat on chairs in the shade of trees, children ran through and around the groups, yelling, laughing and in general having fun.

A man in stained blue coveralls, holding two hot dogs, was talking with another man also in coveralls. Ben doubted they had attended the church service, but no one seemed to mind their presence. In fact, Angela Beattie approached the coverall-clad men and Ben was sure she was offering to get both of them one, if not two, pieces of pie.

"Sorry for ditching you," Shannon said, coming to his side. "Kerry needed a hand cutting up some pies."

Ben looked her way, surprised at the little jolt her presence gave him. She wore a fitted yellow dress with a black leather belt at the waist. The color brought out the reddish tints in her auburn hair and enhanced the sprinkling of freckles on her nose.

She looked like summer.

He was obviously smitten, which, to his surprise, was okay with him.

"I've been busy while you were gone," he said. "Pete, the real-estate agent, offered to show me some houses. I just got offered not one, but two pieces of pie by Mrs. Beattie."

Shannon's laugh was like a little gift making him think he might actually be funny.

"Looks like she's working on Cliff Rubinski,

as well," she said as she lowered herself to the empty lawn chair behind her.

"You know him?" Ben asked as he joined her. "Something tells me neither he nor his friend came to church this morning."

"He doesn't go to church, but he shows up at every church event. Looks like he and Drake just came off the job."

"I suppose you know what he does?" Ben asked.

"He and Drake drive gravel trucks for the Fortuin brothers. They're doing some work on Coal Creek Road."

As Shannon returned the wave of a young girl with a pink streak in her hair, he asked, "So who is that girl?"

"Lacy Miedema. Works at Mug Shots. You should know that."

"I've only been there a couple of times." He glanced around the crowd. "So let's see how good you really are at this." He zeroed in on a prospect. "How about that older man sitting at the table with my mother and your nana. Glasses. Has a cane. Wearing the straw fedora."

"Too easy. Nicholas Anderby and he's the grandfather of that young boy over by the gazebo who's flirting with the girl who looks like Julia Roberts." Shannon's eyes flicked over the gathering. "The Julia Roberts lookalike is the daughter of the woman at the pie table, who in turn is the sister of that lady playing with the little kids at the playground, who is—"

Ben laid a finger on her lips, catching the sparkle of fun in her eyes. "I get it. You know everybody."

He removed his finger and she grinned up at him. "I've lived here since I was twelve. I work in the hospital. I've probably treated half of the people here."

While she spoke she nodded at another young couple, who waved at her as they walked past.

"There's something unique about that," he said quietly. "Being so connected to a community."

Shannon shrugged, but Ben could see she wasn't as indifferent to his comment as she seemed. "I'm thinking I might miss this more than I think."

Her casual comment sent a jab of ice through him. Miss this, meaning miss this town when she was gone. He should've known she still had her plans in place.

And why should she change them? He had no definite objectives and while things were so fragile between them, he didn't dare offer her an alternative.

Did he?

"I'm surprised you still want to leave a place

that is such a part of you," he said, trying to sound as offhand as she was. It was a valid question after all. "There's community here and a real sense of people watching out for each other. I think that's hard to walk away from."

Shannon wrinkled her forehead, as if weighing his words. "I heard a comedian once say people move away from their hometown because it's the only way to outrun your nickname." Her hand came up and twirled a tendril of hair around her finger. "Maybe it's also a way to leave your reputation."

He hesitated a moment, but decided to plunge in and lay the past out on the table. "What reputation are you trying to leave, then?"

She kept slowly twirling, her eyes seeming to look backward into her past. "Jilted bride."

The words came out quietly, but Ben could see the pain they caused her.

He couldn't stand it and took her hand in his, turning him to face her. "You know you are so much more than that. That is not who you are unless that's how you see yourself."

Shannon's smile was gentle, as if humoring him. "Maybe, but it's also how people perceive me. At the wedding I overheard a girl…heard her wonder why I took you to the wedding a year after your brother dumped me."

"Don't you think that might simply be a

throwaway comment? Just an offhand observation? Some retelling of the history of this town?" He pointed to her knee. "If someone asked you, in a couple of months, how your knee is, which looks really good by the way, would you think they see you as The Girl Who Cut Her Knee, or would you think it's merely some piece of information they have on you. Just like you know Lacy Miedema works at Mug Shots and Cliff Rubinski drives a gravel truck and likes to come to church events even though he doesn't come to church."

Okay, that was a speech and a half, but he couldn't stop once he got going. And the pensive look on Shannon's face was encouraging.

"Not that long ago you told me about the two parts of ourselves. How we see ourselves and who we want to be. I think I should add to that. How we think others see us. I think your perception of how others see you is not reality."

She nodded hesitantly, as if in agreement but still unsure. "You might be right."

"So how do you see yourself?"

Shannon tightened her grasp, then looked down at their joined hands, as if trying to find an answer there. "I used to see myself the way I think the town does. I used to think I was the poor girl that got left, not quite at the altar, but within striking distance." She laughed lightly, then looked up at him again. "That's changing, however."

He hardly dared hope it was because of him, but as their gazes held he sensed it might be.

"And, as an addendum to the whole identity issue, I don't think of you as Arthur's brother anymore, either. To me you're just Ben Brouwer. Well, not *just* Ben Brouwer, I mean only Ben Brouwer," she added with a self-conscious laugh.

A light breeze picked up and swirled around them as if erasing all the doubts and concerns that had hung around them the past while. Relief slipped through Ben, and he felt he and Shannon had come to an important turning point. Now they could move on without constantly looking over their shoulders at the past.

"Ben Brouwer is what my passport says," he joked.

"While we're talking about identity," she continued, "I think you need to acknowledge exactly who you are, as well."

"We've already talked about me," he said with a light laugh. So much for leaving the past behind. She was determined to bring this part of his past up repeatedly.

"Well, yeah, but I don't think the issue was resolved," Shannon said quietly.

Silence drifted up between them, an easy,

comfortable silence, broken by the shouts and laughter of the people around them.

The community that Shannon knew so well. The community he felt a yearning for.

"The local hospital desperately needs another doctor," she said, pushing on. "And a doctor is who and what you are. You've tried to push it aside, but I can tell you haven't been able to suppress that part of your identity."

Ben tried not to squeeze her hands too hard as his old emotions and frustration washed over him. "I told you how much I sacrificed to become a doctor, how much I lost. I don't know if I'm able to face the sorrow that is part of being a doctor."

While Shannon listened she made lazy circles with her fingers over the backs of his hands, traced a scar he'd gotten as a resident when a patient he'd been treating went ballistic and the scalpel Ben had been using flew up and landed on the back of his hand.

The patient, a young man who had overdosed on drugs, died five minutes later.

Shannon stopped her tracing, then lifted her hand. "See that young girl over there? The one on the teeter-totter wearing the blue baseball cap?"

Ben heard the question in Shannon's voice, then looked over to where she was pointing.

A girl of about seven was laughing as the sun glinted off the blond hair flying around her face. He recognized her, but couldn't place her.

"Her name is Tracy Thomas. Her father was one of the guys who stood up for Carter and Emma. She came into the E.R. a couple of months ago, choking. Dr. Henneson had to do an emergency tracheotomy. Saved her life. Because this is a small town, it's common knowledge so I'm not breaking any privacy laws, by the way. Anyone can tell you that story—she's told it herself enough times. Will even show you her scar." She glanced around some more, then pointed to a dark-haired teenager sitting off on his own. "Eugene Dorval came in with a gash in his neck and had lost a lot of blood. He could have died, but Dr. Shuster pulled him back from the brink. Again, common knowledge." She turned back to him, her expression earnest. "I know you said you made many sacrifices to be a doctor and you saw too much death, but here you get to see the results of the good things you do. You get to see the mother whose daughter you saved, the husband whose wife you saved, the families and the friends. Yes, we've lost people and, yes, we've seen sorrow, but we get to see so much joy and happiness and fulfillment, as well." She turned to him. "These are all parts of the job, too. In Ottawa you probably didn't get to see the lives you saved so you can only think of the lives you lost. But I know, for a fact, that you saved more lives than you lost."

The passion in her voice called to him, igniting a spark of hope.

"You said you made many sacrifices for your job and I know you feel personally responsible for Saskia's death. I want you to think of all the other sacrifices you made to get to where you did. Can you really turn your back on those, as well?"

Ben held her earnest gaze and the spark flickered and grew. As he looked around the gathering he again felt the yearning that had been growing of late. The desire to be a part of a community. The desire to be anchored somewhere.

Why not here? Why not doing what he had trained for and, as Shannon had said, made so many sacrifices to do?

"I'll think about it" was all he could say.

"Do that. You would be welcomed with open arms. I think this is a good place for you. I think you could heal here."

He smiled as he pulled her to her feet. "What about you? Could this still be a good place for you?"

A shadow flitted over her features, but then she gave him a shy smile. "I'll think about it."

Still holding his hand, she walked toward a group of people engaged in earnest discussion. "Now let's go meet some more of the good people of Hartley Creek and find out what Bob Clark and Evangeline Arsenau are having such a lively chat about."

Hailey stopped at a shop window on Main Street and tilted her head to one side, studying the mannequin on display. "What do you think? Does that look like a teacherly outfit?"

Shannon glanced at the hot-pink skirt and bright orange halter top displayed in the window of Threads, a woman's clothing store. "Do you want to blind your future students?"

"You might be right," Hailey agreed, as she started walking. "I have to say I'm a bit nervous about having my own class this fall after working as a teacher's aide for the past few months."

"You'll do fine," Shannon assured her, slowing down to check out the selection in the window of Chocoholics.

Hailey caught her by the arm and pulled her along the sidewalk. "Don't even think about it. Because if you go in, I'll go in and I want to make sure I won't be waddling down the aisle."

Shannon felt the tiniest flash of envy at her sister's future plans, but it was mingled with a deeper happiness that Hailey and Dan had found each other again. "You won't be waddling. You'll look lovely."

Hailey shot her sister a concerned look. "So, how was Carter and Emma's wedding for you? I mean, she used lots of the stuff you were going to use for your wedding, as well as the same hall."

"You know, it was fine."

"You and Ben seemed to be enjoying yourselves at the wedding. I think you danced every dance with him."

"It was fun."

"Fun? Ha." Hailey poked her in the side. "Pretty lame word for what I think happened. When you and Dr. Ben came back to the hall after your little trip down to the river, you floated into the room."

Shannon knew better than to give her sister any reason to continue so she said nothing. She also knew her heated cheeks would give her away.

"You're blushing," Hailey crowed as she held the door open to Mug Shots.

Shannon had been promising Hailey they would get together for lunch. The time for Shannon to leave was fast approaching and Hailey said she wanted to get as much quality time in as possible.

The café was quiet as they stepped inside

so she and Hailey had their pick of places to sit. Hailey led the way to the low-slung leather couch parked by the window overlooking the street.

"My favorite spot," Hailey exclaimed in delight, balancing her coffee cup and plate holding her sandwich. "Now we get to see all the comings and goings."

"Because there are so many of them in Hartley Creek."

"There's enough," Hailey retorted. "Sit here long enough and something will happen."

Shannon laughed, got herself settled in and took a bite of the delicious panini.

While they ate she and Hailey's conversation covered Dan and his daughter, Natasha, Hailey's upcoming teacher's job at the school this fall. Their sister Naomi and her dying fiancé and Naomi's eventual return to Hartley Creek. Nana and her health.

Family, community—the things that mattered, Shannon thought as she wiped her hands on her napkin.

Thankfully Hailey said nothing about Shannon's upcoming job or when she would leave.

The bell above the door tinkled again and a couple of young boys came into the café to flirt with Lacy Miedema and order a couple of cups of coffee. Before they left, they glanced Hailey and Shannon's way and gave a quick wave.

Shannon wasn't sure whether they knew Hailey or her, but it didn't matter. Small-town friendliness in action.

"So, now that we got all that other stuff out of the way," Hailey was saying as she wiped her hands on her napkin and turned to her sister with a grin, "let's get back to Ben."

Shannon preferred not to. She wasn't sure what to think and what to feel.

"He seems to care about you," Hailey was saying as she set her plate and cup on the table beside the couch.

"How would you know that?" Shannon asked, taking a sip of her tea.

"Okay, even before the whole him-taking-you-to-the-wedding thing, that time I came to the house with cupcakes he couldn't keep his eyes off you." Hailey leaned back in the couch and tucked her foot under her, settling in for a chat.

Shannon didn't reply to that.

"At the church during the wedding? I had a good vantage point and could see him watching you most of the service. And we won't even talk about the dancing."

"Then don't," Shannon said, looking down at the steam rising from her mug.

Hailey was quiet and Shannon shot her a side-long glance, hoping she hadn't hurt her sister's feelings. But Hailey's grin was proof she hadn't.

Then Hailey grew serious. "You're allowed to be happy, you know," Hailey said. "I don't think you need to get all hung up on the whole issue of him being Arthur's brother."

Shannon pursed her lips, as if thinking. "You know, that's not even an issue. Not anymore."

"Okay. That's neatly out of the way. Why are you holding back?"

Shannon took another sip of her tea, giving herself time to formulate thoughts she wasn't even sure she had organized in her own mind.

"I have my plans—"

"It's not like working in Chicago has been a life's dream of yours," Hailey interrupted, adding an abrupt wave of her hand as if wiping away Shannon's objections.

"No. But it is still part of my future plans, which, I might add, are coming closer and closer." She took a slow breath. "I'm not sure I'm willing to change everything because of… because of a man."

"You know I was in the same situation with Dan," Hailey replied.

Shannon lowered her cup to her lap, cradling it between her hands. "You and Dan had a history. You used to date. Ben is just…well…"

"He's Ben. He's attractive. He came to church with you and you two seem to have something kind of special going on. What's the problem with that?"

"It's more than that." Shannon put her cup down and turned to Hailey, folding her arms over her chest. "You weren't as old as I was when Dad left, so I don't know if it had the same effect. I was left behind twice. Once by Dad and once by Arthur. I don't know if I dare take a chance again. I don't know if I have the reserves to take that risk."

Hailey's expression grew serious and she laid her head sideways against the back of the couch. "I remember Dad leaving. I was only eight, but I remember watching him packing up his suitcase then walking past me and out of the house. I felt helpless and unable to do anything. Plus, Mom moved out shortly after Dan's brother died and so did Dan. So don't think you're the only one who knows about being left behind."

Shannon heard the latent pain in her usually happy-go-lucky sister and it tugged at her heart. "I'm sorry, Hailey. I wasn't trying to make it look like I've had it so much tougher than you or Naomi. It's just, after Dad, I felt like I was in charge of cleaning up behind him. Mom wasn't much help and you were, as you said, only eight. After Arthur left, I was also in charge of the cleanup. I was the one who had to cancel the caterer, the flowers, the minister, the deejay, the hall, figure out what to do with table favors for two hundred people, decorations and all the other stuff." Shannon caught herself as remnants of the old bitterness seeped into her voice. That was almost a year ago. She had moved on.

Hailey's expression softened and she reached over and took her sister's hands in hers. "I never knew," she said softly. "I'm sorry I didn't do anything to help you."

Shannon squeezed Hailey's hands in return. "That's because I didn't ask. Big-sister complex blended with a heavy dose of pride." Their gazes held for a few more heartbeats and Hailey's smile grew melancholy.

"And you still have the dress."

Shannon thought of it, then laughed lightly. "Mostly because I didn't know what else to do with it. In a town the size of Hartley Creek half of the single girls in town had already seen it and who wants to get married in a bad-luck dress?"

"The only person with bad luck was Arthur for walking away on you."

"That doesn't matter anymore," Shannon said. "Ben made an interesting point. He was married, too, but he and his wife divorced. He told me that at least Arthur spared me that and he is right. Better a broken engagement than a broken marriage."

Hailey nodded her agreement, then released her sister's hands and leaned back again.

"So where does all this leave you and Ben?"

Shannon caught a wisp of hair and twined it around her finger. "I think… I think I'd like to see where it goes. I think I really care for him. I don't know if I dare change my plans."

"Do you care for him the same way you cared for Arthur?"

Shannon took her words and weighed them, then shook her head. "No. I've known Ben for less time than I've known Arthur, but I can tell that Ben is much, much different. What I feel for him is deeper somehow. Wider even."

"Which makes it scarier, too, doesn't it?" Hailey asked.

Shannon nodded.

"I think you need to pray about this," Hailey said. "I also think you need to be open to where God is trying to bring you. Don't let your plans get in the way of something wonderful."

Shannon heard the wisdom in her sister's voice, then expelled a deep sigh.

"I think you're right," she said.

"I usually am," Hailey replied with an airy wave of her hand. "You didn't sign a contract with the hospital in Chicago did you?"

"Not yet."

"So call them. Tell them that you're postponing your arrival."

"That seems irresponsible."

Hailey leaned closer and grabbed Shannon's hands. "I was in the same position as you. I know how scary this might be. But please, don't give up on Ben because of a job you don't need."

On an intellectual level Shannon found herself resisting Hailey's encouragement. She had told the hospital in Chicago she was coming.

But her heart—oh, how it clung to the hope Hailey spoke of. The possibilities.

"Don't overthink this, sis," Hailey said. "Give Ben a chance. It's worth it."

Shannon let Hailey's encouragement take her along. "Okay. I'll call them this afternoon. Tell them to give me a month."

Hailey grinned. "A lot can happen in a month. My goodness, a lot can happen in a week." Then she glanced at her watch. "I better get scooting. I promised Natasha I would take her to the library after lunch."

They bussed their cups and plates, but as they left Mug Shots, Hailey reminded her sister to make the phone call before she and Ben went out for the evening.

The thought of her date with Ben quickened Shannon's heart and her steps. She was going to spend time with Ben. And it was okay. As Hailey told her, she didn't have to think so far ahead.

Even as anticipation sang through her, tendrils of misgiving crept up. She brushed them aside. It would be okay. Everything would be okay.

It had to be. Her heart couldn't take the blow of being left behind again.

Chapter Eleven

The cool night air carried with it the sweet scent of the lilies growing against her nana's house. The streetlights cast a watery glow over the street, creating intimate shadows on Nana's porch.

Shannon couldn't help a tremor of anticipation as she and Ben made their way up the walk to the veranda.

At the door, Shannon turned to Ben and smiled. His eyes were a glitter of black, his smile a slash of white.

"Thanks for a wonderful evening," she said, clasping her hands in front of her. "I'm glad we decided to forgo the movie."

"I'm glad I wore sensible shoes," Ben said with a gentle laugh.

The crowd of young kids and the movie listed on the marquee had made Shannon doubt how much she and Ben would enjoy the movie. So she had suggested a walk through town on the new trail the chamber of commerce had completed a month ago.

It had taken them longer than she'd expected, but then, they hadn't maintained a blistering pace. Hand in hand, they had meandered down the gravel path, along the river, up to the golf course, through the newest subdivision and then back along the old train bed beside the park to arrive back at Ben's truck three hours later.

The whole time they walked their long strings of conversation had taken as many turns as their feet had. They talked about movies they had seen, books they had read, places they wanted to see. They shared ideas, they even shared work stories, each from their own perspective.

Best and most important of all, they talked about their faith. She discovered that while Ben had held on to his beliefs all through med school, it was his internship and his subsequent work in the E.R. that had tested him.

Since coming to Hartley Creek he had felt as if his heart, overwhelmed and empty, had slowly been refilled. Nourished.

Now they were back at the house and the evening was over. Shannon was exhausted, but she didn't have to work until two the next day, so she had time to catch up on sleep.

Ben, she understood, was finally helping his mother rearrange the furniture. That was as far as his plans went.

"I hope you're not too tired," Shannon said, glancing down at Ben's feet as if to make sure.

"I've been on my feet longer than this," he said. "I'm sure you have, too." Ben fingered a lock of hair away from her face, then let his hand drift down to cup her cheek. "But you've got to admit, this was much nicer," he said, his voice growing husky. Then, to Shannon's surprise and delight, he bent over and followed the touch of his finger with his lips.

A shiver danced down her spine and when he drew away, all she could do was smile.

"I have to agree," she said, her voice breathless. She laid her hand on his chest and then, stepping up on tiptoes, brushed a kiss over his mouth in return. "Much, much nicer," she said.

Ben chuckled and gently drew her in his arms, holding her close. "So what shifts are you working the next few days?"

"I have four twelves starting at three o'clock tomorrow, and then I'm off until Monday."

After she had called the hospital in Chicago, she had immediately let her boss at Hartley Creek Hospital know she was available for a few more shifts. They had given her whatever she could work.

"Why do you want to know?" She was fairly sure she knew the answer, but she wanted to play the coy girlfriend. Just for fun.

"I have some plans," he said, brushing another kiss over her forehead. "I was thinking of an excellent Thai restaurant in Cranbrook that Carter said you loved. Figured I might need someone like you to help me make exactly the right menu choices. I hate food regret."

"Food regret is one of the worst kinds." She slipped her hand up his chest and let her fingers linger at the warmth of his neck. "I'm sure I could help you avoid that horrible situation."

"That's great," he said with a light chuckle. "I'm sure we'll see each other over the next few days. We can firm up plans as the week goes by."

"Sounds good."

An easy, comfortable silence rose up between them. In the background Shannon heard the rhythmic croak of frogs, the hoot of an owl on the hunt, the muted swish of cars driving on the main street two blocks over.

But her attention was riveted on Ben. His expression had grown serious, his eyes glittering in the dark.

"You're a very special person, you know," he said, his voice pitched low. Intimate.

His words resonated through the empty spaces

of her life, filling them with emotions she didn't think she would feel again.

Better emotions. Purer emotions.

Then he lowered his head and caught her mouth with his, his lips moving gently over hers, drawing out her own response. When he moved away it was as if all the breath had been pulled out of her body.

She rested against him, her head tucked under his chin, her hand still holding on to him. "You make me feel as special as you say I am," she replied, her voice muffled against his shirt.

He stroked the top of her head with his chin. They stayed close to each other awhile longer; then Shannon reluctantly pulled back. "I should get to bed. Need my beauty rest."

"Not that badly," he chuckled, gently releasing her. "You're amazingly beautiful already."

"I'll take that compliment," she said with a smile, folding his words up in her mind, storing them up, along with the other memories of tonight, for later when she was alone.

"Have a good sleep," he said, brushing the back of his hand over her face.

Shannon nodded. Then, fighting her impulse to move closer, she turned and slipped inside the house. She closed the door behind her, then leaned against it, resting her head on the wood, letting the events of the evening seep into her soul.

She heard his footfalls echo on the wooden steps, then nothing, and she assumed he was cutting across the lawn to his mother's house.

Turning, she took a quick peek through the window beside the door only to see him looking back over his shoulder at the house, as if hoping to catch another glimpse of her.

When he tossed off a quick wave, she knew he had seen her and in reply she waggled her fingers back. Then he turned and jogged across the lawn, his long legs easily closing the distance.

She bent over, slipped her shoes off and slowly made her way up the stairs in her bare feet.

When she turned on her bedside lamp she wondered if Ben could see. Wondered if he was watching her window. The thought warmed her heart and made her feel protected and comforted.

She changed, then slipped into bed and took her Bible off the end table. The Bible her nana had given her to remind her of where her hope lay.

Nana had given the gifts with the unspoken hope that Shannon would change her mind about moving away. The only change Shannon had made was to postpone her move, and now she was postponing again.

Had she done the right thing?

Shannon put the question aside. She wasn't sure what she could allow herself to think. For now she knew Ben was growing more important to her and slowly becoming a part of her life.

While the thought gave her pause, she knew she needed to take the chance. She thought of Hailey's comments about not letting her plans get in the way of something wonderful. Plans that grew hazier the more time she spent with Ben.

Shannon settled back in her bed and turned to where she had stopped reading last night. She had been reading the Psalms and tonight it was Psalm 23, the Shepherd Psalm.

Though the words were as familiar to her as her face, she read each word carefully, slowly, letting the Psalm refresh her soul.

The Lord is my shepherd, I lack nothing. He makes me lie down in green pastures, He leads me beside quiet waters, He refreshes my soul, He guides me along the right paths.

Shannon truly felt that for the past few days she had been led beside quiet waters. Her life had come through the valley of shadow and she had arrived at a good place.

She finished reading, set the Bible aside and let her prayer of thankfulness rise up to God.

No second thoughts attacked her when she was done. And as she snuggled down into her bed and pulled her blankets around her, she could still feel Ben's arms holding her close.

Feel his lips touching hers.

Thank You, Lord, she prayed. *Thank You for this man. I pray that I can let go of my fears and allow him into my life.*

She waited a moment, then turned off the light, rolled onto her side and let sleep claim her.

As the door of the administrator's office of Hartley Creek Hospital fell closed behind him, Ben fought a last-minute burst of nervousness.

Had he done the right thing? Was he thinking clearly?

He took a step away from the door, glancing at the envelope of paperwork required of him.

He had made sure to come when Shannon wasn't working. For some reason he wasn't clear about, he didn't want to run into her. He was fairly certain Daphne, the nurse he had met when Shannon had cut her knee, would fill Shannon in on all the details, but for this moment the decision was his and his alone.

Please, Lord, he prayed, *Let me make the right decision for the right reasons.*

The involuntary prayer surprised him yet gave him a measure of peace.

He glanced around the hospital again, quiet now. The pervasive scent of disinfectant brought back a sense of expectation. Things happened in this place.

Even as he formulated this thought, he heard the familiar wail and caught the strobing light of an ambulance as it pulled up to the doors.

The quiet and peace fled as the doors flew open and the paramedics burst into the hospital, joined by a nurse and one of the doctors Ben had just met.

Symptoms and jargon chattered between them, a rapid-fire balance of information and questions.

"...Cyanotic and dyspneic."

"Possible pulmonary embolism."

He had to stop himself from running over and joining in as he recognized the symptoms the paramedics rattled off. A jolt of dismay flashing through him. Guy might not live.

Death. Again.

But right behind that came Shannon's comment about choices and how it was his job to deal with what was at hand.

He also thought of the people she had pointed out at the picnic and the lives that had been saved. The lives that bore witness to the work done in this very E.R.

He waited until the paramedics, nurse and doctor were behind the curtain of the E.R., then slowly walked toward the door.

He shot a glance over his shoulder as he left. He missed this, he realized. Missed the energy and the challenge. Missed the shot of adrenaline that came with challenging cases and the race against time.

He missed being a participating member of society and missed using the gifts given to him.

He pushed the door open and stepped into the sunshine, then walked toward his truck, drawing in a long, steadying breath. The hospital was located at the edge of town, close to the highway, and yet, even from here, the ever-present mountains stood guard.

A group of kids drove by on their bikes, laughing as they raced each other toward the ice cream store. A car pulled up and a young mother stepped out, opening the door and taking a little girl out of the car seat in the back.

Ben could see the strain on the mother's face as she clutched her child close, hurrying to the emergency department. He wanted to rush over to her side, ask what the symptoms were, see what he could do, but she was already down the stairs and had stepped through the doors before he could respond.

Another time, he reminded himself, feeling the responsibility of his work.

Shannon had been right, he thought as he unlocked his truck. He was a doctor. Now, if he decided to take the offer, he was going to be a doctor in Hartley Creek.

He knew Shannon was sleeping right now; otherwise, he would have phoned her to talk to her about it. That was okay. A much better time to discuss it would be tonight over dinner.

The thought of their date put a smile on his lips and a cliché spring in his steps.

"So, no food regret?" Shannon teased, reaching across the wooden table of the restaurant and stroking his hand.

"You are a genius," Ben said, smiling as he captured her fingers in his. "And this place is deserving of our patronage."

Indeed, the ambience of the place added to the food experience. With low ceilings, subdued music, globe lanterns and fanciful Thai decorations with their bright colors on the walls and tables, he felt as if he and Shannon had been immersed in another culture.

And the food…

"I'm glad you enjoyed it," she said, her fingers tracing gentle circles on the back of his hand.

"We'll have to come here again," he said.

"Good idea, but there are a lot of restaurants in Hartley Creek we have to eat at yet. Sabrosa's has excellent Mexican food and the Curry Bowl is always, always worth a visit. Never mind the Lost Mitten. Or the Royal if you want the best burger you've ever eaten."

Ben grinned at her enthusiasm.

"Sounds like we'll be busy for the next couple of months."

"Always something to look forward to in Hartley Creek," she said quietly, giving him a gentle smile.

He leaned forward and stroked her cheek. Things had become so comfortable between them the past week. A couple of days ago, when she'd come off her shift, he and his mother had had dinner with Shannon and her grandmother. The next night she had been invited to his mother's place.

He'd cooked and she'd been properly impressed. Always a good thing.

"So now that you've finished the yard work, do you have any new projects?" Shannon asked.

"I'm running out of things to do. I don't imagine your grandmother has any new jobs for me?"

Shannon shook her head, her eyes glinting in

the dim light. "I'm sure she could come up with something, but for now, I think she's willing to simply enjoy being in the house."

"It's nice for her that you're there."

Shannon nodded, looking distracted. "It is, but I have to make a decision about my living arrangements fairly soon."

He guessed she was talking about her job in Chicago.

Questions hovered, waiting to be voiced, but he held back. Though he knew things were shifting and changing between them, growing more serious, he was still unsure of what he was allowed to expect from the relationship.

What he was allowed to say.

Shannon glanced up at him, a question in her eyes. He held her gaze and decided to take a chance.

"You could stay in Hartley Creek," he said.

She tilted her head to one side, her smile growing. "I suppose I could. If I had a good reason to."

He swallowed, old fears and pain rearing up, warning him. But he pushed them down. He had paused and hesitated and evaded long enough. For too long he had let circumstances dictate what he would do.

It was time to step out in faith.

Sending up a quick prayer for courage and strength, he began.

"I'm hoping that I can…" Still, he hesitated, and in that moment Shannon's phone rang.

He pulled back, annoyed at the interruption.

When he looked down at the call display on her phone lying on the table beside their joined hands, his annoyance shifted to dread.

The number on the screen was Arthur's.

Shannon frowned at her phone, then, pulling her hand loose from Ben's, snatched her phone up. She leaped up from the table, turning away from Ben as she hurried away.

Her eagerness sent a warning chill down his spine and he felt a flurry of emotions riffle through him. Pain, anger, frustration and, worst of all, fear.

Why was his brother calling her?

And why was she so eager to be alone to talk to him?

He sat back, his heart thumping heavily in his chest. He had come so close to making some kind of declaration. The next move in the relationship. Some basic commitment to staying here and encouraging her to rethink her plans based on his feelings for her.

He dragged his hands over his face and sucked in a long, slow breath, gathering his scattered emotions.

So close.

Shannon was back remarkably quickly, her face flushed and her eyes bright with what? Anticipation? Joy?

She slipped into her seat and dropped her phone into her purse, avoiding his gaze.

He didn't want to think too deeply about that.

Thankfully the waitress came by right at that moment. "Will you be wanting anything else?" she asked, her smile bright as she glanced from Shannon to Ben.

Ben shook his head. "Just the bill, please."

His curt tone erased her friendly smile and for a moment he regretted speaking so abruptly. But what could he say?

The woman I am falling for is still infatuated with my louse of a brother?

He pulled out his wallet, not even looking across the table at Shannon, not sure if he wanted to see the happiness on her face. Not sure he wanted to know how excited she was to be hearing from his brother.

The drive back home was quiet, Ben's mind chasing a dozen thoughts and catching none of them.

His brother had called Shannon. The ex-fiancé of the woman he'd hoped would be willing to see him as more than a boyfriend.

He had come perilously close to asking her to make the next move in the relationship.

He glanced over at Shannon, but she was looking out the window, as if she couldn't face him. On the one hand he wanted to know what was going through her head.

On the other, not.

As they came through the tunnel, Ben thought again of the picture Shannon had showed him in the rocks. The Shadow Woman. Waiting for her lost love to return.

Was that Shannon?

He pushed the doubts to the back of his mind. He was being paranoid. Just because his brother had called, didn't mean Shannon would welcome him with open arms.

You don't know for sure what's going on. Ask her.

He couldn't. Not as long as she sat in the truck, silent, clutching her phone as if clinging to the remnant of the conversation she'd had with his brother.

By the time they got to her grandmother's house, tension gripped his neck and he felt as if he were reliving some of his less memorable high school dates.

The ones where no one dared say anything because neither dared be the first one to take the risk and potentially be shut down.

He dutifully walked around the truck, opened her door and let her out. She didn't take his hand as they walked to her grandmother's veranda, but when they got to her grandmother's door, she turned to him, laying her hand on his chest.

"Thanks for a lovely evening," she said quietly, smiling up at him. "I had a great time. I hope you did, too."

"Fantastic," he said with forced enthusiasm. He wasn't completely lying. He'd had a great time until his brother's phone call. His mind ticked back to the dress still hanging in her closet and he wished he could dismiss it.

He couldn't because the dress was still there, a physical reminder of what Shannon had lost. A reminder that she couldn't let go.

Her smile shifted, as if sensing his reticence. "Well, have a good sleep," she said quietly, shifting away from him.

He wanted to pull her close, kiss her again, chase the doubts beating like moths against his tired brain.

Instead he took her hand in his and received a wavering smile. "I better go. Got a busy day tomorrow. Lots to do." He waited a moment to give her a chance to make the first move. To show him something.

"One other thing. That morning concert at

the park tomorrow?" she asked, "I have to bail on you. Something else has come up."

"I thought you didn't have to work," he said, throwing out the comment casually. As if he didn't suspect Arthur was the reason she was canceling.

"I don't" was her cryptic response.

Ben's heart faltered at her evasiveness, but there was nothing more to say.

"Okay. That leaves me free to do some of the things I've been wanting to do." He waited a few seconds, giving her one more chance to make some move, give him some idea of where her heart lay.

She stood with her head bowed, braiding her fingers together. She was so beautiful, and though his heart ached, he couldn't stop himself.

He caught her by the shoulders and gave her a quick kiss then released her. "Goodbye, Shannon," he whispered. "Hope things go well for you."

Then he turned and left, doubts and worries and Arthur's shadow chasing him back home.

Chapter Twelve

So now what was he supposed to do?

Ben looked at the paperwork he had gotten from the hospital. Paperwork that was required before he could be hired. He'd been trying to read it for the past hour, but the words simply wouldn't register.

As he shuffled through the papers, all he could think about was Arthur calling Shannon.

And Shannon going to meet his brother today.

In itself that wouldn't have bothered him. What concerned him was he only knew this for certain because his mother told him. He and Arthur hardly every spoke, which was the fallout of lives moving on completely different trajectories for so long. But that Shannon hadn't said anything about the date stung.

You don't know if it's a date.

What else could it be? She and Arthur had

a long history. Shannon still had the wedding dress in her house, as if she couldn't let go of that relationship.

Ben dragged his hands over his face and tried to focus on the papers in front of him. Did he really want to do this if Shannon returned to Arthur?

The door from one of the guest rooms down the hall creaked open and Ben glanced at the clock. His brother was up earlier than he had figured.

Why shouldn't he be? He had a hot date with Shannon.

"Hey, bro, I'm home," his brother called out.

When Ben had come back from seeing Shannon, it was to a note from his mother saying Arthur was coming back tonight. Wasn't that nice?

Really nice, Ben had thought. Now his brother was awake and Ben had to pretend he was happy to see him.

Ben gathered up the papers on the table and shoved them in an envelope. He didn't want his brother or his mother to see even an inkling of his plans.

As he got the last papers in, his brother walked into the kitchen, whistling, grinning from ear to ear. His blond hair stuck up in all directions, and though Ben knew he hadn't come in until late last night he still looked fresh and bright-eyed.

"Good to see you, man," Arthur said, grabbing his brother's hand and pulling him close for a manly hug. His brother gave him two thumps on the back, but then Ben quickly pulled away.

Arthur had never been much for shows of affection, but then neither was Ben so he couldn't complain.

"So, you're looking a lot better than the last time I saw you," Arthur said, his one hand still on his brother's shoulder. "I heard you're not working as a doctor anymore, either. Whats with that?"

"I had stuff going on."

"Yeah. I heard about Saskia. Sorry, bro." Arthur was quiet for a few seconds, as if contemplating life and death, but very quickly his smile returned. Serious moment was over.

"Heard you got a lot done here for Mom," he said. "Got any other plans?"

Ben fingered the envelope in his hands. "I've got a few irons in the fire" was all he said. There was no way he was telling Arthur his plans. Not when his brother looked so pleased with himself. "What about you? How's the new car dealership working out for you?"

"Fantastic. Got top salesman of the year again, so I'm thinking it's time to branch out.

Start up my own business." Arthur leaned back against his mother's countertops, shoving his hand through his hair, and just like that, it was neat again. "Got a good reason to."

"What do you mean?" Ben gave him a frown, not sure he wanted to hear what Arthur had to say.

"I'm meeting Shannon this morning."

"Yeah. Mom told me."

"She's a great gal and I still can't believe I did what I did to her. I'm going to tell her that, too. I don't blame her if she can't forgive me, but she's such a sweetheart, I'm sure she will." Arthur punctuated the comment with a grin. "I'm hopeful."

"Okay. That's good, I think."

Arthur's expression grew serious. "You don't sound happy about that."

Ben replied with his own laconic shrug. No way was he getting all kiss-and-tell with his brother. Thankfully it sounded as though their mother hadn't said anything to Arthur. That was a small mercy at least.

"Anyway, I thought I'd stick around for a bit after I see her," Arthur continued. "I've got a few plans, but I want to see how things go between us. I heard she was moving to Chicago. She's got a job there. I think it's a fantastic idea. So we'll see how things progress."

Ben tapped the envelope he held against his leg, feeling suddenly foolish about his own plans. His mind ticked back to last night. The palpable reserve surrounding Shannon after Arthur's phone call. Now Arthur's ebullient spirits.

And what was he going to do about that?

What could he do?

"That's good you're staying around," he said with forced enthusiasm. "I was thinking of heading out into the mountains for a couple of days. Do some hiking. If you're sticking around I don't have to worry about Mom being on her own while I do."

He was making things up as he went, but he had his reasons.

He didn't want to be a spectator to any potential reunion between Shannon and Arthur if, indeed, things went as well as Arthur hoped.

And if Shannon truly still yearned for Arthur, he didn't want to get in the way.

"That's a great idea," Arthur said. "You could use some time to yourself. You've been busy working your fingers to the bone on Mom's place and Nana Beck's place." Arthur sighed. "You always were the more responsible one."

Irritation surged through him, but he quashed it. Yes. He'd been the one to do Arthur's dirty work and now he was making it easy for Arthur to potentially break Shannon's heart again.

You don't know that.

Ben thought of the intimate moments he and Shannon had shared. The reality was he had known Shannon for a far shorter time than Arthur had. And Shannon and Arthur had history. Maybe his brother only needed to grow up. Maybe Shannon needed to give him another chance.

"Anyhow, I have to get to the outfitting store to pick up some supplies," Ben continued, pleased he could sound so casual. "After that I'm heading directly into the hills."

"But I just got here," Arthur complained. "We've got a lot of catching up to do. I was hoping you could give me some ideas of how to convince Shannon—"

"Sorry, Arthur. I had this planned before you came." Which wasn't technically a lie. When he'd first come to Hartley Creek he had bought a book on backcountry hiking trails. He'd been meaning to do some hikes and had a few planned, but then he got involved with Shannon and started working on Mrs. Beck's house and those plans got put on the back burner. "Besides, the weather is really good now and they're forecasting showers in a couple of days so I figure now's as good a time as any."

"Then we'll see you when you get back.

Maybe I'll have some news for you," Arthur said with a grin.

"Maybe" was all he said, saluting his brother with the envelope.

Then he strode down the hall to his room and closed the door behind him. He leaned back against the door, his emotions in a turmoil.

Okay, Lord. I'm doing the right thing here. I'm giving my brother and Shannon space to figure out where they're going. I wish You would help me find where I'm going.

He looked at the envelope again, thinking of all the things Shannon had told him. Maybe he'd still apply. Maybe he'd still work here.

If he was doing it, he would do it for himself.

And Shannon and Arthur?

According to Arthur, Shannon was going through with her own plans so she would be gone anyway.

He was a doctor, he thought, setting the envelope on his dresser, thinking of what Shannon had told him. She was right. He missed his work, missed being a part of something important. Something bigger than himself.

Before he made any final decision, he needed some time alone.

In record time he had his clothes packed up in a knapsack. As he put the last sweater into the bag, his eyes fell on a Bible sitting haphazardly on a stack of books. He picked it up and put it inside, as well. May as well take some quality reading material.

Besides, he and God needed some catch-up time, and where better than up in the mountains he couldn't stop looking at?

When he got back to the kitchen, Arthur was sitting at the kitchen table eating a bowl of cereal and flipping through the *Hartley Creek Herald.*

"So, I'm gone," Ben said. "Could you tell Mom what's happening?"

Arthur got up, wiping his mouth on a napkin. "You sure about this, man? I mean, we haven't had much chance to talk."

Ben wasn't sure he wanted to listen to whatever his brother might have to say. In spite of being each other's only sibling, they had never been close. Arthur was the kind of person who went his own way and if you didn't want to come along, so be it.

"We'll talk when I get back," Ben said. "I really need the break." He clapped his hand on Arthur's shoulder and held his gaze for a moment, trying to get a read on his younger brother.

But he only saw Arthur's blue eyes staring back at him, brimming with optimism.

"You take care, hear?" Arthur said.

Ben nodded, then strode out of the house and down the walk. He tossed his knapsack in the back of his truck. He had to go to one of the outfitting stores in town to get a tent, sleeping bag and some food. Things he'd been meaning to buy for some time now.

Before he got into his truck, he looked over at Mrs. Beck's house. He wondered if Shannon was getting ready for her date with Arthur.

He climbed into the truck, slammed the door and jabbed the key into the ignition. With a twist of his wrist, his truck roared to life and seconds later he was on the main road, headed toward downtown.

And after that, the mountains.

"I made a huge mistake. I know that. I'm such an idiot." Arthur leaned forward, his elbows on the wooden picnic table, his eyes earnest, his voice pleading as he tried to reach for her hand.

His blond hair was artfully arranged, and Shannon was fairly sure he had chosen the blue shirt to bring out the blue in his eyes.

Arthur had wanted to meet at Mug Shots, but Shannon had nixed that plan immediately. She didn't want anyone in Hartley Creek to see her with her ex-fiancé.

So she had chosen this picnic site five miles

out of Hartley Creek, fairly sure not many people would see her here with him.

She looked away from his pleading gaze, down at the table with its myriad of carved initials proclaiming undying love. *Karl loves Deanna. CA and RJ forever.*

She'd never had a junior-or senior-high boyfriend. No one to declare his affection for her by way of a carving or a graffiti painting on any one of the bridges spanning Hartley Creek or the Morrissey River.

She wondered if that was why she had allowed Arthur to sweep her off her feet. He was charming and attentive and had made her feel as if she was the most special woman in his life. At least for the first half of the relationship.

"Before we talk about that, when you called me after you canceled the wedding, you said you had made a mistake getting engaged. So what happened to make you change your mind?"

Arthur sighed, then plunged his hand through his hair, rearranging its waves. "Like I told you, when the wedding started getting close, I got cold feet and I, well, panicked. I'm not the first groom to feel that way."

And you sent poor Ben to do your dirty work. And like the conscientious person he is, he came through for you.

"When I had some time away, I realized I was wrong," he continued, his voice taking on that pleading tone he did so well. "I made a mistake. And when I heard you were still around and still single, I knew I had to come back."

Yes. Poor, desperate, jilted Shannon, pining away for a man who didn't have the decency to tell her to her face he couldn't marry her.

"So there was never another woman?" she asked, knowing she had to.

Arthur shook his head vehemently, his hand clenched on the table. "No. Absolutely not."

Shannon couldn't help a wry smile. Jilted was jilted, but it might have been easier to understand Arthur's reasoning if passion had made him flee the scene. An undying love for another woman he couldn't live without.

Instead it was plain ordinary fear. Mundane second thoughts. Not the stuff of which great romances are built.

"So, do you think there's a chance for us?" Arthur continued. "I did love you and do love you. I know you still care about me. Mom told me you still have the wedding dress."

Mom talks a bit too much.

Shannon dismissed that thought. Sophie was a sweet woman. For all Shannon knew, Sophie had simply passed the information on as just that. Information.

"I'm thinking of giving the dress away," she said.

Her abrupt comment sent a glimmer of fear over his features. "No. You can't. Not when I'm ready to make a commitment to you and to us. You can still use the dress if we get married again." He held out his hand as if offering a great prize she would be crazy to turn down.

Shannon looked at his hand and couldn't help but compare it to his brother's.

Though Ben was a doctor, his hands held the scars and calluses of someone who worked. Who made sacrifices.

Arthur's job as a car salesman required that his hands look clean, neat. In fact he even went for a manicure from time to time, something Shannon used to tease him about.

"And what about Hartley Creek? I thought you didn't want to live here," Shannon asked.

"My mother told me you got a job in Chicago."

Now it was Shannon's turn to look puzzled. "Is that part of the reason you're willing to take a second chance with me? Because I'm moving away?"

Arthur pulled back, looking offended. "We fought about you staying here. I wanted to leave and you didn't. So, now that you're moving, it removes a huge barrier to our relationship. And Chicago. What a great choice. I've always wanted to live there."

Shannon narrowed her eyes, as if trying to get this man in focus, as if trying to see what had once attracted her to Arthur. Yes, he was good-looking and, yes, he was charming, but he was also inconsistent and confusing.

The polar opposite of his older brother.

Warmth flowed through her at the thought of Ben.

"I hope that happy look on your face means you're thinking this through," Arthur said, lowering his voice. He gave her his most charming smile and, for a moment, Shannon saw the man she had been attracted to.

At one time she had thought of him as kind, caring and attentive. And he had been. He had sent her flowers, had called her frequently when he was away. They'd had fun together.

But that was another time in her life and she had moved on.

Now she had Ben.

A throb of uncertainty marred the moment, but memories of the times she had spent with Ben wiped them away. She and Ben had shared more openly with each other in the few weeks they had known each other than she and Arthur ever had.

Arthur may have given her tangible gifts—flowers, jewelry, cards for no reason. But Ben had given her much more. The gift of openness. Of raw honesty.

And, almost as important, the gift of trusting her with the dark secrets in his soul.

"I don't really have anything to think through," she said quietly, folding her hands in her lap and glancing down at her watch as she did. She wanted to get back home. Back to Ben. Then she looked over at Arthur, whose face still held that expectant look. "We had fun and we had our time together," she continued. "But something made you realize we shouldn't get married and I think you need to respect that decision. You and I were not meant to be together and it's not happening."

"Have you found someone else?" His voice held an accusatory tone that made her want to laugh. As if Arthur had any right to demand information on her current love life.

But her feelings for Ben made her feel magnanimous and Arthur may as well know sooner rather than later. He was, after all, Ben's only brother.

"I've met someone who is very special to me. We… I care about him. A lot." Still, she hesitated. Speaking the words aloud made it real and public.

And open for humiliation if nothing further came of it.

What else could she do? Hide? Cower behind past hurts? As Ben had said, she was her own person. Her identity was not tied up in whom she was with, but who she was.

"Someone from town?" Arthur pressed.

"Someone from your family. It's your brother. Ben."

Arthur couldn't have looked more stunned than if she had slapped him.

"Ben? Dour, cranky old Ben?" He gave his head a tiny shake as if to let the information fall into the right slot. "Why him? He's kind of grumpy."

Arthur's confusion would have been comical if it wasn't for the fact that it smacked of arrogance.

"Ben is a very caring man who has had to deal with a lot." Shannon eased off her defense of the man she cared so much for. Arthur was his brother and if he couldn't see Ben's good qualities, Shannon wouldn't be able to change his mind.

"Well, yeah, I know, but he's so dark. And he's divorced," Arthur added, as if this comment alone should make her have second thoughts.

The only acknowledgement Shannon gave him of that unreasonable comment was a quick nod. "Anyway, that's the way things are and I thought you should know."

Arthur slumped down, heaving a deep, heartfelt sigh. "So that's it? You and me? Nothing?"

"Sorry, Arthur. We had our chance, but we both know it wasn't working toward the end anyway. It's better this way."

Arthur gave her a world-weary smile and once again, Shannon caught a glimpse of the man she had thought she loved.

"So if things work out between you and Ben, please don't expect me to dance at your wedding," he said quietly as he got up.

Shannon didn't want to think that far. Didn't dare.

"For now, let's say we'll probably see more of each other than we have the past year" was all she would say.

Arthur came around the table and laid his hand on her shoulder. As she looked up at him, the sun shone through his blond hair, haloing his head. He really was an attractive man, she thought. Only not so attractive all the way through.

"You know we had a really good thing," he said, his hand tightening on her shoulder.

Shannon covered his hand with hers, feeling pensive when he leaned over and dropped a light kiss on her head.

"You're a wonderful person, Shannon." Then with another light squeeze, he released her and walked across the grass to his car.

Shannon turned to watch him go. Each step he took away from her was like a loosening of a thread holding her to her past. And when his car pulled out of the parking lot, she felt it snap.

She waited for a few more moments, relishing the peace washing over her in gentle, lapping waves. Though she had dreaded talking to Arthur, for the first time in months, she finally felt truly free of him and of the hold he had over her emotional state.

Thank You, Lord, she prayed as a gentle breeze wafted over her like a tiny blessing.

Then she got up and, with light feet and even lighter heart, fairly floated to her car.

She was going to see Ben.

"All Ben said was that he would be gone for a few days?" Shannon forced a smile as she asked the question.

Sophie Brouwer, looking as confused as Shannon felt, simply nodded. "He called me this morning. Told me he was hiking up Hartley Pass, said not worry and that he'd be back in a couple of days. He also told Arthur." Sophie pulled the fronts of her orange jacket around herself, giving Shannon a baleful look. "He didn't say anything to you?"

Shannon shook her head, struggling to keep her smile intact. She and Ben hadn't made definite arrangements for today and she knew she had made it sound as if she was busy, which she had been. But she'd wanted to get the whole Arthur thing out of the way before making any plans with Ben.

Now Ben was gone and he hadn't said anything to her about leaving, let alone leaving for a couple of days.

"Did he leave any message for me?"

Sophie's expression grew more morose, and Shannon swallowed the rising panic in her chest.

"No, sweetheart. Nothing." Sophie reached out as if to touch her, then pulled her hand back. "I'm sorry. My sons aren't very good to you, are they?"

Her words chased a chill down her spine. What was she trying to say?

Shannon gave her a wan smile, said goodbye. Then, as she trudged back to her house, Ben's last words to her rose up like an apparition.

Goodbye, Shannon. Hope things go well for you.

Why had he said goodbye? Was he leaving her?

And why not? That's what the men in your life do.

She pushed that thought aside as she entered the house. Not Ben. He wasn't the type. He was a solid, caring man.

In the few weeks they'd known each other, she'd felt as if she had gotten to know Ben much better than she'd ever known Arthur. Ben made her feel as if she could give him something.

Then why was he gone?

"Did you find out where Ben is?" Nana called out from the kitchen, where she was making lunch.

"Sophie only said that he left" was all Shannon got out as her throat thickened.

Her nana came out of the kitchen and stood in the doorway. "Didn't he tell you where he was going?"

Shannon shook her head. "It doesn't matter. I've got...other plans."

"Are you still coming to my book-club meeting day after tomorrow?" Nana asked, concern lacing her voice.

"Yeah. I am."

She didn't have much heart for it, but she had promised. "Sorry, Nana, but I'm going upstairs for a nap," she told her grandmother, knowing this was the best way to get Nana to leave her alone.

Nana just nodded, then scurried into the kitchen. As she made her way up the stairs, she heard her nana talking on the phone in a quiet undertone.

Shannon closed the door behind her, shutting off her grandmother's conversation as her gaze flicked around her bedroom. *Isn't this just great?* she thought. *This is all I have to show for my years of work? Still single and living with my nana?*

She sat on the bed and covered her face with her hands. What kind of loser was she? Why couldn't she hang on to the men in her life?

You don't know what happened. Wait and see.

But the voice of reason was drowned out by the flurry of questions and worries beating at her resolve.

Why did he leave without talking to her? What had he meant when he said goodbye? Also, that other comment—*hope things go well for you.* Those weren't the things you said to a girlfriend. That was the language of leaving.

A language she was far too acquainted with.

She lay back, staring up at the ceiling, self-pity hovering on the edges of her consciousness.

You don't know how long he will be gone because he didn't want to tell you.

Shannon pressed her hands to her heated cheeks, wishing she could still her anxious thoughts. Wishing she could put Ben's leaving in the right place in her life.

She took a deep breath, then pushed herself up, reaching for her Bible. A source of comfort and wisdom. She turned to the bookmark she had put in the pages the last time she'd read.

Tonight she would be reading Psalm 25. Why not now?

In You, Lord my God, I put my trust. I trust in You; do not let me be put to shame, nor let my enemies triumph over me. No one who hopes in You will ever be put to shame. Shannon stopped there, her finger resting on the last word as the tears of shame she promised herself she wasn't going to shed slipped down her cheeks.

Shame. She had lived with it so long. Had let it define her. Now, with the silence from Ben resounding through her life, once again she was letting a man define who she would be.

She turned back to the Bible and read on.

Show me Your ways, Lord, teach me Your paths. Guide me in Your truth and teach me, for You are God my Savior and my hope is in You all day long.

She let the words seep into her soul as a sense of surety washed over her. She was God's child. That's where her identity was. That's where her hope lay. She thought Arthur had visited shame on her life, but she had let it take over and had let that event overcome the most basic truth of her life.

She was Shannon Deacon, child of God. Her hope was in God and nothing else.

Whatever happened to her now she had to put into the perspective of who she was and where her hope lay.

Even as the words of comfort stole into her soul, she felt an ache for what she had almost had.

Help me to trust in You. To put my identity in You, she prayed. *Help me to cling to You, Lord, and Your promises.*

She clutched the Bible, as if to let the words, by osmosis, seep into her life and become a part of her essence.

She didn't need Ben. She didn't need Arthur. She only needed her Lord.

Chapter Thirteen

Shannon trudged to the kitchen, her feet aching and her head pounding. She had just come off one of the twelve-hour shifts she had taken on to fill her empty days.

Each beep of her phone sent her heart into overdrive, but she'd heard nothing from Ben.

No text. No call.

It was like Arthur all over again.

Each evening her nana would put food in front of her, a concerned look on her face, and each evening Shannon made a game effort to get it down.

Each evening she returned to her Bible and each evening received strength from what she read.

She thought of how long it had taken her to get over Arthur and took comfort from that. She'd gotten through that; she would get through this.

The thought was cold comfort. Because she knew losing Ben was a much deeper, harder blow. She and Ben had talked about things she had never spoken to Arthur about. In the short time she had gotten to know Ben, she'd learned he was a better man. And she also knew he was a better fit for her.

And now this?

She dropped her purse on the kitchen table and saw the note from her nana propped up against the fruit bowl.

Soup in the fridge. Don't forget that you promised to come to book club tonight.

Shannon discharged a weary sigh as she glanced at the clock. She didn't feel like heading out in an hour. Not after a long, hard shift at the hospital.

Yet, part of her knew she needed to, to put her past with Arthur behind her for good.

While the soup heated up in the microwave, she went upstairs and changed from her scrubs to street clothes. She could have a shower tonight when she got back. She glanced in the mirror above her dresser and made a face at her reflection. Minimal makeup, hair still pulled back in a utilitarian ponytail.

Then she waved her hand at the mirror as if

dismissing what she saw. What did it matter? Book club was just a group of women.

She tucked a loose tendril of hair behind her ear and as she did, caught the reflection of the gold nugget hanging around her neck.

She fingered it a moment, thinking of August Klauer, how he had chosen to come back. And Ben? Would he come back?

Shannon closed her eyes, trying to understand what she should feel. She knew she cared deeply for Ben and his leaving without contact hurt her more than it should have.

What would the people of Hartley Creek think? She had skipped church on Sunday, choosing to work instead so she could avoid questions about where Ben was.

She let go of the necklace and took a deep breath.

Please, Lord, help me to find my trust and my identity in You, she prayed as she walked to her closet.

As she pulled open the door she heard the swish of the plastic garment bag hanging from the back. She pulled it down and held it out at arm's length, her gaze flicking up and down the dress.

A brief image of Ben, standing in the door of her apartment while she wore this same dress, flitted into her mind and she wondered what he'd thought then. How he'd seen her.

Had he pitied her?

She quashed the memory, then folded the dress over her arm and headed down the stairs. Supper and then book club and then this chapter of her life was over.

Ben finally switched his phone on before he made that last turn onto the highway leading into Hartley Creek. He had needed the time away, time to think and clear his head. And though he was sure the reception up in the mountains was nonexistent, he didn't want the distractions of his cell phone.

He had spent time walking, thinking, praying and trying to figure out what he had to do next. He knew his thoughts would be clearer away from the distraction of Shannon and Arthur and the questions surrounding their possible reunion.

And though he was unsure of Shannon, he at least had come back from this trip much more sure of his calling. As Shannon had told him, he had made many sacrifices to become a doctor and many sacrifices since then. His job had come with a cost, but he knew not being a doctor would cost him more in terms of his identity. He knew he had poured too much of his energy into the job before, but at the same time it was an important job.

And it was a job he could do here in Hartley Creek. His mother was here and he had slowly been finding community, something he hadn't found in his years in Ottawa.

When he came back into town, the first thing he would do was go to the hospital and talk to the administrator.

He held up his phone, glancing at the number of messages showing up on the screen. He pulled his truck over to the side of the road, trying to stifle a trickle of apprehension as he checked the ten messages on his phone.

His mother. His mother again. Dan at the hardware store. Arthur simply asking Ben to call him back. His mother again with some obscure message asking him to please come to book club tonight if he came back on time. It was important.

Nothing from Shannon.

What did you expect? You walked away from her.

To give her and Arthur space.

Oh, very self-sacrificial. Did you ask her if that's what she wanted?

Ben stilled the accusing voice. He had made his decision out of respect for Shannon. If she wanted him in her life, he figured she would let him know.

And if she didn't?

His heart turned over at the thought, but he clung to the words from 1 Corinthians 4 that he'd read while he was in the mountains. Words that reminded him of his own responsibilities.

Now it is required that those who have been given a trust must prove faithful.

He had been given the trust of his skill as a doctor. He was good at what he did. Now he had to be faithful with what he had been given. He didn't know where Shannon fit into all of this. For the moment he simply had to do what lay in front of him and what was required of him.

As he turned onto the street his mother and Mrs. Beck lived on, his eyes flew to Mrs. Beck's house. Shannon's car was still parked at the curb.

And Arthur's was gone.

Were they out together?

He pushed the questions aside, grabbed his stuff and was about to head toward his house when the door of Mrs. Beck's house opened.

Then Shannon stepped out.

He frowned. She wasn't with Arthur.

And as she came down the walk, he noticed she was carrying a garment bag. The same bag that held her old wedding dress.

She was frowning as she walked, digging in her purse for her keys and then, when she got them out, she looked up.

Directly at him.

She halted midstride and her keys slipped out of her fingers onto the ground. She didn't pick them up. Instead she just stared.

Ben felt his heart downshift. Then, before he realized what he was doing, he had dropped his knapsack and was walking toward her, drawn by the longing he saw in his gaze.

"You're back," she breathed, her hands trembling.

He wanted to ask her a hundred questions, but instead, bent over to pick up her keys. She'd had the same idea and they met, kneeling on the ground, their hands tangling as they grasped the keys at the same time.

Ben yanked his hand back as Shannon picked up the keys. Then, as she straightened, she lost her grip on the garment bag.

Ben caught the bag and Shannon let go a nervous laugh.

"I'm all thumbs today," she said.

Ben still held the bag, looking from her to the dress and then back to Shannon again.

"I'm guessing this is your wedding dress?"

She nodded as she took it from him. "I'm bringing it to book club. Nana was telling me about a young girl that joined them. She's getting married and can't afford to buy a new dress."

Ben blinked as her words registered. "You're giving it away?"

She nodded, shaking out the bag and settling it over one arm. "I don't have any use for it."

He looked at the dress again, recognizing what it symbolized

"I thought...you and Arthur...he wanted you back." Even as he stammered out the words, hope kindled deep in his soul.

"He didn't get me." Her words were abrupt, almost harsh. "I'm not something to be put down and picked up at will. Ignored when inconvenient and then paid attention to when the time is right."

The bitterness in her words were like a lash. As if she was including him in her indignation with his brother.

"I'm not sure what you're saying," he said, holding her narrowed gaze.

Shannon shifted her feet, the garment bag rustling as she did so. "Why did you leave?"

Through the accusation in her voice he caught a note of dismay. Disappointment. And something he hardly dared acknowledge.

Sorrow?

"I left to give you space."

"For what?"

Ben sighed as a sudden breeze swirled around them as if picking up on Shannon's agitation. He tried to hold her gaze, but she stared down at the keys she held in her hands, her knuckles white.

"I saw Arthur before he took you out that morning," Ben said, choosing his words as carefully as he would his instruments. "He sounded so confident. Like he was so sure you two were getting back together again. I knew... I remembered how devastated you were when he left." His gaze flicked to the dress she had bunched over her arm, like it was another item of clothing instead of the symbol of her dreams. "I also didn't know what you and he talked about that night he called you. So I thought if you two were getting back together again, I didn't want to be in the way."

Nor did he want to be a witness to it, but he didn't say that.

Shannon's grip on the keys and the dress loosened and as the breeze died down a sigh slipped past her parted lips. "He phoned to ask me to meet him. To talk to him." Then she looked up at him and the embers of hope that had kindled began to glow. "I agreed because I wanted to be done with him. I wanted that part of my life over."

"Is it?"

She pressed her lips together and nodded, then looked up at him. "I learned a lot about myself in the last couple of days. The main thing is that my identity is not defined by who I am with. My identity is in Christ."

She spoke the words with a ringing authority that both encouraged him and, at the same time, raised a niggle of doubt.

"So you don't need anyone in your life? You don't need me?" he asked.

She looked up again, into his eyes, as if searching for the right answer to give him.

"I don't know how to answer that. When you left, I thought it was a repetition of all the other times I've been left. I still don't know what to think."

Her cautious response ignited the embers of hope. He took the keys from her hand and dropped them into his pocket, then folded her hand in his. "I didn't only leave to give you and Arthur space, I left to give myself time to think. To make sure I was making decisions for the right reasons. I want you to know I've decided to stay in Hartley Creek and take the job in the hospital."

Her eyes flew to his and her smile grew as her hand tightened on his. "That's wonderful. I'm so glad."

"It's a big step for me, but I'm sure I'll be

okay." Then he lifted her hand to his lips and brushed a kiss over her knuckles. "But I know I'd be more than okay if you were here."

"What are you saying?" Her voice was breathless, as if she hardly dare ask for confirmation.

Ben glanced down at the wedding dress hanging at half-mast over her arm, a symbol of other lost dreams. He gently removed it and laid it on the grass; then he stood, took both her hands in his and looked into her eyes.

"I'm saying that I don't want to live here without you. I don't want to spend the rest of my life without you. I know you've heard these words before but I'm hoping that you'll believe they mean more this time than they ever have. I love you. And I'm hoping that you are willing to trust that I am a man who keeps my promises."

Shannon closed her eyes and Ben saw tears drifting down her cheeks.

He couldn't stand it anymore. He pulled her close and then, taking another chance, captured her mouth with his. She melted against him and her arms captured him and held him close.

All doubts fled and second thoughts were quelled by their embrace.

Ben was the first to pull away and he tucked Shannon's head against his neck, his stubbled chin resting against her hair.

"I love you, Shannon Deacon, and I promise

I won't leave you willingly." He tightened his hug. "I want to spend the rest of my life keeping that promise."

Shannon clung to him for a moment longer, then drew away. "I like those kind of promises," she said quietly, reaching up to cup his chin in her hand. "And I make the same promise. I'll never leave."

Ben looked down at her, his heart full, hardly daring to believe that they were together, all misunderstandings swept away.

For now it was just Shannon and Ben and the promise of a future together.

He touched her necklace, his smile rueful. "August Klauer made the right choice when he came down that mountain to stay. I know I did, too."

Shannon covered his hand with hers, her smile as bright as the sun that shone down on them like a blessing on their promises.

"I'm glad you came back."

"Even though I smell like smoke, need a shave and a shower and a change of clothes?"

Shannon laughed at that. "I'm sure August Klauer didn't smell a whole lot different and I'm sure Kamiskahk didn't care, either." As if to prove it, she stood up on tiptoes and kissed his stubbled cheek.

He caught her hand, his eyes searching hers as he grew serious.

"And are you going to be okay with staying in Hartley Creek?" he asked, needing to be assured the shadows in her life had been banished.

"More than okay," she said, her smile serene. "If I'm with you."

He dropped another kiss on her forehead.

Then the wind picked up and lifted the dress up, tumbling it across the grass. Shannon pulled away and in a few steps captured it. She returned to Ben, a pensive smile curving her lips as she looked at her watch. "I'm supposed to meet that girl in a couple of minutes." She paused, glancing up at him, her hand adjusting the folds of the garment bag.

Ben read the unspoken question in her eyes and even though he still smelled like wood smoke and needed a shave and a shower, he took the garment bag from her hands. "Why don't I come with you? My mother left some message on my phone about coming to book club tonight. Said it was important."

"That would be great," she said, relief tingeing her voice.

"Can we take your car?" he asked. "My truck is kind of dirty. Don't want to mess up the dress."

"No problem." Shannon rearranged the dress,

then bent to retrieve her dropped purse. "I have to find my keys now."

Ben dug into his pocket and pulled them out. "I've got them," he said, holding them out to her. "I'll trade you for that dress."

She took the keys and handed him the clear, plastic garment bag.

He held it out at arm's length, examining the dress with a critical eye.

"Something wrong?" Shannon asked.

"Nothing's wrong. I just remember picking this dress up off the sidewalk when you moved in and wondering why you still had it. Now it's leaving. Best thing that ever happened to this dress." He flashed Shannon a smile as he walked to the car. She opened the back door. He laid the dress on the seat and shut the door with a decisive thud.

She looked from the dress to him, and then suddenly she caught him by the arms, reached up and kissed him full on the mouth.

"What was that for?" he asked, pleased, but surprised at the impulsive gesture.

She ran her hands up his arms, letting her hands rest on his shoulders. "You are a good man, Ben Brouwer. I'm so thankful for you. You've made my life fuller and richer. You healed my soul."

Her words were like silvery fragments of

happiness lacing his heart. He stroked her face again, cupping her cheek.

"And you healed my heart," he said, his voice faltering a moment.

She blinked, then cupped his face in her hands. "I'm glad," she said, punctuating her comment with another kiss.

He smiled down at her, then took the keys from her hand. "I suppose we should get going. Your nana is going to wonder what is taking you so long."

"So is your mother."

Ben frowned as things clicked into place like tumblers on a combination lock. "So your nana arranged for you to bring this dress to the girl at book club tonight?"

Shannon nodded, giving him a puzzled look.

"And my mother calls me, practically begging me to come to book club, as well."

He could see Shannon had figured it out, too.

"They wanted you there when I gave the dress away."

"They just don't quit," Ben said with a light laugh.

Shannon flashed him a quick grin. "I'm glad they didn't."

Ben stroked her cheek with his knuckle, then gave her another smile. "Me, too." Then he swung the keys around his hand. "So, I guess we should get down to the Book Nook so they can see how this story ended."

"Or began," Shannon said.

"Or began," Ben agreed.

They got into the car and drove away, into the sunset and into their new beginning.

* * * * *

Dear Reader,

We live in a tight-knit community and I know firsthand that there are few secrets. People seem to know everything about everybody. There are advantages and disadvantages to that. The disadvantage is that, if, as with Shannon, something embarrassing and humiliating happens, everyone knows it and talks about it. And as the person who is embarrassed, you can feel that this is the event that defines you.

But not all the talk is harmful. True, gossip does happen and not all of it is kind, but for the most part when people talk about the things that happen in the community it's because people care. Our family has dealt with some truly hard times and each time our community has been there for us. I'm thankful for the strength we've received and if, when we left the room, people talked about us, that's fine, too.

I hope you enjoyed this part of the Home to Hartley Creek series. Shannon will probably show up again and you will be able to see how far she's come on her own journey.

Blessings,

Carolyne Aarsen

P.S. One of the best parts of my day is getting letters from readers. If you have anything you want to ask me or tell me, please write me at caarsen@xplornet.com Or you can visit my website at www.carolyneaarsen.com

Questions for Discussion

1. What was the theme of this book? How do you think it applies to your life?

2. What did Shannon mean when she told Ben that sometimes you have to leave town to lose your nickname?

3. How did you feel about Shannon's initial reaction to seeing Ben again?

4. Why do you think Ben struggled with guilt over his wife's death?

5. What were some of the reasons Ben didn't see himself as a doctor?

6. Why do you think Shannon saw herself the way she did? Have you ever had to overcome a perception of how you see yourself? How did you do this?

7. How did you feel about Nana Beck and Sophie Brouwer's meddling in the relationship? Have you ever done anything like that?

8. What was your reaction to Arthur's actions at the end of the book?

9. What challenges will Shannon have to overcome to have a fulfilling relationship with Ben?

10. What did you see as the biggest obstacle to Ben and Shannon's future relationship?

LARGER-PRINT BOOKS!

GET 2 FREE
LARGER-PRINT NOVELS
PLUS 2 FREE
MYSTERY GIFTS

Love Inspired

Larger-print novels are now available...

LILP11B

Love Inspired® SUSPENSE

RIVETING INSPIRATIONAL ROMANCE

Watch for our series of edge-
of-your-seat suspense novels.
These contemporary tales
of intrigue and romance
feature Christian characters
facing challenges to their faith...
and their lives!

AVAILABLE IN REGULAR
& LARGER-PRINT FORMATS

For exciting stories that reflect traditional values,
visit:
www.ReaderService.com